HUBERT INVENTS THE WHEEL

HUBERT

INVENTS THE WHEEL

CLAIRE & MONTE MONTGOMERY

ILLUSTRATIONS BY JEFF SHELLY

WALKER & COMPANY
NEW YORK

First published in the United States of America in 2005 by
Walker Publishing Company, Inc.
Distributed to the trade by Holtzbrinck Publishers

For information about permission to reproduce selections
from this book, write to Permissions, Walker & Company,
104 Fifth Avenue, New York, New York 10011

Library of Congress Cataloging-in-Publication Data

Montgomery, Claire, 1951–.
  Hubert invents the wheel / Claire & Monte Montgomery ;
illustrations by Jeff Shelly.
     p. cm.
  Summary: A creative fifteen-year-old boy in ancient Sumeria
invents the wheel, resulting in many adventures, both humorous
and threatening.
  ISBN 0-8027-8990-0 (hardcover)
  [1. Wheels—Fiction. 2. Sumerians—Fiction. 3. Inventions—
Fiction. 4. Humorous stories.]   I. Montgomery, Monte, 1957–
II. Shelly, Jeff, ill.   III. Title.

PZ7.M7643Hu   2005
[Fic]—dc21   2004061160
            ISBN-13 978-0-8027-8990-7

Book design by Jennifer Ann Daddio

Visit Walker & Company's Web site at www.walkeryoungreaders.com

Printed in the United States of America

4   6   8   10   9   7   5

For our dads, Carl Ermatinger and D. J. Montgomery,
who were always interested in how stuff works
—C. M. & M. M.

To my wife, Christine
—J. S.

HUBERT INVENTS THE WHEEL

ONE

Five thousand years ago—give or take a millennium—if you wanted to move a heavy object, you couldn't use a wheelbarrow, because they hadn't been invented yet. For the same reason, you couldn't use a cart, a wagon, a train, a car, a truck, a plane, or Federal Express.

You had to use a sledge.

A sledge is like a sled: a rectangular platform mounted on two wooden runners. But unlike sleds, which are used by fun-loving children for sliding down snowy hills, sledges are dragged across dry ground by hardworking beasts of burden, such as oxen and onagers.

We'll get to what onagers are in a minute.

Everything about sledges bothered Hubert: their primitive appearance; their massive weight; the grinding sound they made as they scraped along hard, bumpy roads; and, especially, the sad looks they produced on the faces of Meg and Ed, his father's oxen, as they strained to pull a heavy load.

But what bugged Hubert the most about sledges

was that if he didn't come up with a way around it—and soon—he was doomed to go into his dad's business: Gorp's Towing & Hauling. After that, sledges would be his life.

The problem was, five thousand years ago there weren't a whole lot of career choices. You were either a laborer, a farmer, a hunter, a gatherer, or a hunter-gatherer. But mostly, you were a laborer.

Gorp owned his own business, but he was still a laborer. Hard worker, good provider . . . but, frankly, not the brightest guy in the world. For that matter, he wasn't the brightest guy in Mesopotamia (Hubert's region) or Sumeria (Hubert's country) or Ur (Hubert's city). Come to think of it, he wasn't even the brightest occupant of Hubert's house, a one-story, mud-brick bungalow on the outskirts of town. Grading on IQ alone, Gorp probably came in third, after his son and Hodja, but above Spike. Spike was a lizard. Hodja was an onager.

Okay, onagers. An onager is sort of a scaled-down horse, about the size of those miniature ponies at county fairs, but faster, smarter, stronger, and often a lot grouchier. Hodja was Hubert's best friend in the world.

The title of "brightest occupant of Hubert's house" had been held by Hubert's mother, Samarra, until she was lost in a tragic umbrella mishap several years before. Samarra could think circles around the rest of her family, but she loved the whole gang just the same, especially her husband. Gorp was strong, devoted, honest, and gentle, and she liked how he looked with his shirt off, his powerful shoulders flexing as he trudged up the path after a hard day of towing and hauling.

Gorp missed his wife so much that he never even thought about getting married again. He had his job, his house, his oxen, and his son, and he was reasonably content with things the way they were.

Hubert was different—not just from his dad, but from everybody. He was what is now called "creative," but at the time was just called "weird."

Hubert took after his mother. They both had a keen eye and a wild imagination. They were both often unsatisfied with the status quo. And most importantly, they were both inventors.

At the moment, Hubert was in his bedroom inventing a mousetrap.

"See, Hodja, the way it works is, the mouse walks up this little ramp and into the box," he explained. "When he takes the bait, it'll pull on this string, which releases the catch, which triggers the spring. And the ramp flies up and becomes the lid, see?"

Hubert spent a lot of time in his bedroom, which also served as his workshop, studio, and, when Gorp was on his case, hideout. Inventions in various stages of development were all over the place: a palm-leaf fan, a bamboo pogo stick, a rope ladder, an underwater breathing tube, tree-climbing spikes, a wooden hat. He was always working on a bunch of projects at once.

The mousetrap, which was about half the size of a cigar box, was very cleverly designed. Hubert took a screwdriver from his toolbox and made a tiny adjustment to the spring he'd created. The spring had to be strong enough to keep the mouse from escaping, but not strong enough to squash it if the door slammed on its little body. That would be disgusting.

Hubert's toolbox was his most valued possession. His mom made it for him when he was little, filling it with tools she'd made herself: hammer, screwdriver, chisel, saw, file, hatchet. He carried the box around so much that the wooden handle was nearly worn through, but he could never quite bring himself to replace it.

"And these airholes will let the little dude breathe until we can release him back into the wild," Hubert continued. Hodja was glad to see his friend show such concern for a fellow animal; but the fact was, Hubert wasn't as interested in mice as he was in technology.

"Technology" is a long word because it describes a lot: inventing things, building things, perfecting things, fixing things, making hard jobs easier, making unpleasant jobs unnecessary—generally, coming up with stuff that makes life better.

But what Hubert liked best about technology was the way it made him feel. Creating something that did what it was supposed to do gave Hubert the kind of thrill that an athlete gets when she sets a world record or a violinist gets when he receives a standing ovation at Carnegie Hall.

"And now for the trial run," Hubert said, eyes sparkling in anticipation. "Hey, Spike," he called across the room, "you want something tasty?"

Spike, Hubert's hyperactive green lizard, peered between the bars of his bamboo cage. He'd been watching the creation of the mousetrap all morning, unaware that he'd be called upon to test it.

Hubert opened the cage. Sensing that something exciting was about to happen, Spike ran up Hubert's arm, down his back, around his waist twice, down one leg and up the other, before coming to rest on his shoulder, where he paused and sniffed the air with his quivering tongue. (Lizards smell with their tongues.) Something smelled mighty good.

"That's right, boy. A nice, juicy dung beetle," Hubert said as he carried Spike to his workbench and set him down in front of the trap. The lizard took another sniff, tiptoed up the ramp, and looked into the box.

Hodja stood very still. "The moment of truth," Hubert whispered as Spike crept into the box and pounced on the bait with gusto.

Pow! The lid sprang into place. "It worked!" yelled Hubert, pumping his fist in victory. Hodja pumped his hoof. This was a truly momentous event, at least in the field of rodent control.

But before Hubert could open the trap, Spike, who didn't recognize that he was only part of a harmless experiment, freaked out. Shoving his legs through the airholes, he took off like a bullet.

"Uh-oh," Hubert said.

Running blind, Spike zigzagged into the living room, where he collided with Gorp's terra-cotta spittoon, smashing it into a million pieces. Dad wasn't going to like that. Hubert was right on his tail, but Spike managed to hop up onto a windowsill, where he wiped out a row of vases his mom had made. Dad wasn't going to like that, either.

Spike's next move was straight up the drapes. Hubert made a desperate dive for his tail but missed, bringing the curtains and rod down on his head.

Now Hodja took up the chase. Onagers are just as fast as lizards but have less traction (because of the hooves); so when Spike accelerated around the tight corner into the kitchen, Hodja just kept going straight. He pirouetted across the smooth stone floor, wiping out the dinette set. Dad was *definitely* not going to like that.

The kitchen was the smallest area of the house: a counter, some shelves, and a washbasin. Spike rammed into a high stack of dirty dishes, but Hubert managed to make a diving catch before they all crashed to the ground.

Now loaded down with plates, Hubert watched helplessly as the mousetrap, with four green legs sticking out of it, bounced off the kitchen walls like a pinball. In rapid succession Spike tipped over the trash can, smashed a butter dish, and upended a bowl of eggs, which rolled off the counter and broke, one by one. Slipping in the slimy mess, Hubert back-pedaled frantically all the way into the living room before regaining his balance. Amazingly, he hadn't dropped a single plate.

"Whew, that was close," he gasped—just before the flying mousetrap zoomed out of the hallway and raced straight toward him, with Hodja right behind it. Spike fit between his legs. Hodja didn't. The plates went up in the air. The plates came down. The plates broke.

Spike continued to rip around manically, finally coming to a halt when he tripped over a throw rug and flipped onto his back. Hubert picked up the trap. Sticking out of its holes, Spike's legs were still pumping frantically in the air. "You've gotta admit," he said to Hodja, "the trap held up nicely."

At that moment the front door opened, and there stood Hubert's father. And he wasn't happy. Not by a long shot.

TWO

"I've had it, Hubert," Gorp said later as they straightened up the house. "Had. It. I'm laying down the law. No more improvements. No more ideas. No more—what do you call 'em?"

"Inventions?" Hubert suggested.

"*Especially* none of those."

"Dad, I'm trying to make things better."

"Better? How is this better?" asked Gorp, eyeballing the mess. "Everything was fine the way it was!" He held up the broken leg of one of the wooden dinette chairs. The bark was still on it. "Look what you did! You think these grow on trees?"

"I can fix that," Hubert volunteered; but his dad, focusing on putting the dining-room table upright, ignored him. Hubert sensed a lecture coming on.

"You know, it's high time you got serious about a real career," Gorp said. "After all, you're nearly middle-aged."

Hubert was only fifteen, but his dad had a point. In 3000 B.C. life was nasty, brutish, and short.

"Any other kid would give his right arm to take

over a successful business," he said, holding up his left arm. "A business which, might I remind you, has been in our family ever since man first walked upright. That's over five generations!"

Hubert had been through all this before. "I know, Dad," he protested. "It's just . . . well, I'm just not sure if I'm cut out for towing and hauling."

"That's crazy talk, Hube. Couple of years, you'll be every bit the man I am," he said, popping the dung beetle that had baited the trap into his mouth. Hubert just sighed.

Once the house was back in order, Gorp's mood improved a little. "I'm gonna go hunt us up some dinner," he said, slinging his bow and a quiver of arrows over his back. "By the time I get home, I expect the water jug to be filled. To the brim. And don't bother looking for that toolbox of yours, 'cause I hid it." He patted Hubert on the shoulder. "It's for your own good, son."

"Right, Dad," Hubert said. "Happy hunting."

Water was a big deal in Mesopotamia back then. Though the Tigris and Euphrates rivers weren't far away, most of the land around Ur was desert, and growing crops was an iffy proposition at best. The little spring-fed well behind Hubert and Gorp's house provided just enough fresh water for drinking, cooking, and their monthly bath.

Every day, Hubert had to climb 77 steps to the

well, fill a bucket, lug it down 77 steps to the house, and pour it into the cistern in the kitchen. Filling the cistern took thirteen trips. That's 2,002 steps, a number that Hubert knew as well as his own age.

Most days, he took his mind off the drudgery by dreaming up more inventions: a lizard-powered loom for making cloth, a boat that could go underwater, a knife that could cut stone, a muzzle that would stop his father from giving so many orders. But to-day, inspiration fell right into his lap—or rather, across his path.

During the night a poplar tree had fallen near the well. Poplars are long and thin, so Hubert had no trouble moving it out of his way. But as he held the slender trunk in his hands an idea started to take shape in his head. As often happened when Hubert had an idea, it began as a mere whim, quickly grew into a hunch, morphed into a notion, and finally emerged as a fully formed concept. Hubert exam-ined the concept from every angle and quickly real-ized that it would work.

But he would need his toolbox.

Fortunately, Gorp always hid it in the same place: bedroom closet, top left corner. That's one thing Hu-bert loved about Gorp—his predictability. In less time than it takes to say "Mesopotamia," Hubert retrieved the box and went to work on his boldest invention yet: plumbing.

After trimming all the branches from the poplar trunk, he split it down the middle and hollowed out a shallow groove in each half. He did the same with several other poplars in the yard (hoping his dad wouldn't notice the missing trees) and joined the half-pipes together end to end with leather strips so that each one would empty into the next. The whole series snaked down the hill to the house.

At the well end he built a small wooden sluice box—kind of a gate for water—that would divert the stream into his new plumbing system. At the house end he slid one of the half-pipes into the kitchen window. (This task was made simpler by the fact that glass hadn't been invented yet; a window was simply a hole in a wall, and would remain so for several thousand more years.)

Now the water would pour straight into the mouth of the cistern.

The whole system was so simple and elegant, Hubert couldn't believe that nobody had ever thought of it before. Then again, this was a civilization satisfied with moving things by dragging them along the ground, so what did he expect?

"All right, Hodja, let's give it a try," Hubert said as he opened the gate. The water filled the first pipe, then the next, and so on, finally pouring into the cistern in a graceful arc. Hodja demonstrated his approval by kicking up his heels and running in circles. Hubert picked up the hated bucket and flung it as far as he could.

He was on his way to the kitchen to check on the cistern when he noticed a loose connection between two of the pipes. While making the repair, he dreamed up more and more uses for plumbing technology. Maybe the pipes could be made of something harder than wood, or more flexible. Maybe they could run underground, or inside walls. Maybe the water could be pressurized so it could be sent long distances, or even up hills. Maybe . . .

Hubert's daydreaming was interrupted by the unmistakable sound of an onager in danger—more specifically, an onager in danger of drowning.

He raced down the hill and looked in the kitchen window, where he saw Hodja up to his neck in water. Spike drifted by in his bamboo cage. The new plumbing system had done its job, all right—too well. The jug had been filled about a thousand gallons ago.

"Don't worry, guys, I'll save you," Hubert shouted as he climbed in the window and dove into his new indoor pool.

Gorp was in a great mood. He'd bagged a wild boar and was toting it home across his broad shoulders. A good-sized boar would feed him and Hubert for a week: roast boar, boiled boar, boar fritters, boar and eggs, and a special dish that his late wife had created just for Gorp: boar fricassee.

"I'm probably being too hard on the kid," Gorp thought as he approached the house. "Maybe it's just a phase he's going through, like teething, or thumb-sucking, or bed-wetting. He'll probably snap out of it and come to his senses and take over the family business, so I can finally retire." Gorp was pushing thirty-five.

He was still occupied with these comforting thoughts when he arrived at his front door. There was a little puddle of water seeping out from underneath it. Strange. He opened the door.

When the ensuing flood subsided, Gorp found himself lying on his back fifty feet from the house, the soggy boar stretched out across his belly. Hubert, Hodja, and Spike lay nearby, all soaked to the skin.

Hubert sat up and saw the look on his dad's face. "I guess this means you'll be hiding my toolbox again."

THREE

The next morning was Monday, which meant work. Hubert and his dad were up before dawn, and by the time the sun rose they were already inching along the road to the capital city of Ur on their sledges. Meg and Ed towed Gorp's heavy superhauler with ropes tied to their horns; Hubert's smaller sledge was pulled by a rope around Hodja's neck.

"Dad, how far would you say we've traveled?" asked Hubert.

"At least half a mile," Gorp proudly replied. "Making good time." He seemed to have put yesterday's incidents out of his mind. This was another of Gorp's good qualities: a short memory.

Hubert was glad to see his father happy again, but he couldn't help frowning when they were easily passed by a duck and her three ducklings. On foot. He decided to raise a risky subject.

"You know, I was thinking, Dad. If we could make these sledges move a little smoother, it'd be easier on

the animals and we'd get to work faster, so we could sleep later."

"You're starting it again," Gorp warned.

"I'm just trying to make our lives easier."

"That's the problem, Hubert! You always want to do things the easy way."

"Well, doesn't that make more sense than doing things the hard way?"

Gorp frowned. Logic confused him. "In our family there's a long tradition of doing things the . . . traditional way. You know. Traditionally."

Now Hubert was getting frustrated. "Mom wasn't like that," he said. "If she were here—"

Gorp exploded. "That's my point. She's *not* here. And why? Because she was a radical."

"I thought she came up with some good inventions."

"There's that word again," Gorp warned.

"What, 'good'?"

"Don't get cute."

The debate was interrupted by the sound of a woman screaming. Gorp leaped off the sledge and sprinted up the road.

A s if hard work, short lives, scarce water, and primitive technology weren't enough to deal with, the people of Sumeria had another major headache: the people of Assyria. At regular intervals bands of rough, tough, unshaven men would swarm down from the mountains to the north and steal crops from the Sumerians' farms. Everything was fair game: carrots, potatoes, beets— even rutabagas.

That's how desperate they were.

One such raid was under way at Omar's farm. Omar was a favorite target of the Assyrians because he was too old to fight very well and his three little daughters were too young. Omar's wife, Gert, wielded a mean broom, though. You had to watch out for her.

Omar was on his front porch, putting up the best defense he could. This consisted of shouting ineffective threats at the four Assyrian thugs who were helping themselves to his turnips and wheat, loading sacks onto a sledge drawn by two big horses. The girls cowered behind their father.

"Get off my land or I'll perforate you," snarled Omar, seizing a pitchfork.

This cracked up the ringleader, a tall Assyrian with only five teeth: three yellow ones and two brown ones. "Ooh, I'm really scared, Mister Farmer, sir," he said, cutting the pitchfork in half with a casual swing of his sword.

When his men had loaded up the sledge with as much loot as it would hold, the ringleader tucked a big melon under each arm and climbed aboard.

"Let's get out of here," he barked, and they all piled onto the sledge. The ringleader gave another five-toothed cackle and shouted over his shoulder, "We'll be back in the fall for the olives." He yelled, "Hyeahh," and shook the horses' reins.

But the Assyrians hadn't counted on one thing: Gorp.

Gorp's third-best quality, after predictability and a short memory, was a keen sense of justice. To be sure, Omar was an old friend of his; but even if he'd been a total stranger, there was no way Gorp would stand by and let a bunch of thieves ride off with a sledge full of hot produce. And when Gorp combined that sense of justice with his *fourth*-best quality—superhuman strength when angered—he became one lean, mean fighting machine.

Gorp grabbed one of the sledge's runners with his callused hands, groaned a mighty groan, and flipped the whole thing over, sending the Assyrians and their loot flying every which way. Before they knew what hit them, Gorp had jammed a melon over one thief's head like a helmet, drop-kicked another into the hog pen, and banged the last two outlaws together like a pair of cymbals.

Seeing that the tide of battle was turning, Omar and Gert and the girls got into the act, repeatedly whacking the bandits with brooms, mops, and fly-swatters.

Hubert arrived on the scene as the Assyrians were fleeing on their sledge, pursued by a hail of turnips. He was gasping from the long run. "What happened?"

"Your father really saved our necks, Hubert," said Omar, slapping Gorp on the back. "Those Assyrians are one nasty bunch."

Hubert looked admiringly at his father, but Gorp's eyes were on the thieves, who were beating a hasty retreat toward the jagged mountains. The steep cliffs were dotted with hundreds of caves, and each cave, as every Sumerian knew all too well, was home to at least one thirsty, hungry, dirty, angry Assyrian.

FOUR

Smack in the middle of Ur, a city of ten thousand people, the Great Ziggurat was going up. A ziggurat is a building shaped like a pyramid but with the sides stepped like staircases. Though it was only about two-thirds completed, it already towered over the city. This was where Hubert and his father came to work six days a week, fifty-two weeks a year, rain or shine. But mostly shine.

The project required a staggering amount of hard labor, but the people of Sumeria made the sacrifice gladly. The Ziggurat was to be an "all-inclusive community center and meeting place," with something to offer everyone. The working mothers were looking forward to a day-care facility; old folks anticipated a luxurious senior center with marble shuffleboard courts; the kids were excited about the new playground and arcade; and the Sumerian Music Appreciation Society had their fingers crossed for a new concert hall.

In order to meet all those demands, the Ziggurat would clearly have to be very, very, very, very large.

And it was.

Near the structure's base was the construction tent, a canvas awning that shielded the foremen, architects, designers, and managers from the scorching desert sun. Plans, drawings, and models were spread out across tables; but at the moment, everyone's attention was on Gorp.

"Those Assyrians were pretty tough customers, sir. I had my hands full for a minute there," he said.

"I see," said Prime Minister Salvo, who was heading up the construction project. "And how many of them did you kill?"

Salvo was the second-most powerful person in Sumeria, just below the Queen. He was tall and gaunt, and sort of slithered from one place to another. When Salvo glided up next to you, it felt as if somebody had slid an ice cube down your spine.

"Well, I didn't actually kill anybody," Gorp answered. "I just roughed 'em up a little and sent 'em packing."

Hubert stepped forward. "You should have seen it, sir. He really kicked butt!"

Salvo sized up the impudent youth and considered having him imprisoned under Section 339 of the Penal Code (impudence in the presence of a prime minister), then decided it wasn't worth the hassle. He turned back to Gorp. "I see. Excellent work. You're a fine Sumerian. A real patriot. What did you say your name was?"

"Gorp, sir," he answered, swelling with pride. "I'm

in the hauling game. That's my baby over there." He gestured toward his dusty sledge, parked outside the tent. Salvo gave it a quick glance. "Ah. You operate the big rigs."

"We're in it for the long haul," Gorp said, putting an arm around Hubert. That was his company motto.

Just then a trumpet fanfare interrupted them, announcing the arrival of the Queen.

Besides being the most powerful person in all of Sumeria, Queen Eridu was also the most glamorous, the best-dressed, and—by far—the most superstitious. She never made a move without first consulting her Court Astrologer, her Tea Leaf Reader, her Palm Reader, her Phrenologist, her Soothsayer, her Assistant Soothsayer, and her Deputy Assistant Soothsayer. Something as simple as planning a picnic required a careful analysis of recent signs and omens. If Jupiter was rising, or a black dog had been seen standing on a white rock, the Queen packed her wicker basket; if, however, Mars was descending, or a white dog had been seen sleeping on a black rock, she wasn't going anywhere.

She had the utmost respect for the paranormal.

As Queen Eridu made her grand arrival outside the construction tent, riding on an ornate throne carried by the four Royal Throne Bearers, all the workers bowed low. She acknowledged the gesture with a flick of her slender wrist. The Throne Bearers delicately lowered her to the ground, and she alighted and approached her Prime Minister.

"Queen Eridu," he said. "You're looking quite lovely today."

"Thank you, Salvo. And how is our Ziggurat progressing?"

"Magnificently, Your Highness. According to my foremen, if the weather cooperates, the structure should be completed in a little less than seven years."

"Outstanding! That's two years ahead of schedule."

"Your Majesty," he said, "Gorp, here, is one of our laborers. He was just telling of a savage attack by a battalion of Assyrian soldiers."

Gorp dug his big toe into the dirt, leaving a sizable hole. "Uh, it wasn't a whole battalion, ma'am. Just some hooligans, y'know. . . ."

But Salvo, whose chief purpose in life was to manipulate the Queen, was bent on exploiting this incident. He grabbed Gorp's thick arm. "Citizen Gorp managed to drive the infidels back up into the hills. At least for the time being," he added ominously.

Queen Eridu went all jellylike inside whenever she saw a guy with really big biceps, and Gorp's were the size of coconuts. "Gorp," she said. "What a charming name. Tell me, Gorp, what is your sign?"

"My sign, Your Majesty? You can read it yourself. It's right there on my sledge. 'We're in it for the—'"

"No, no," she tut-tutted, "Your *astrological* sign. You see, I'm keenly interested in the celestial realm."

This was a lot of syllables for Gorp to process, but he got the picture. "Oh, right. I think I'm a . . . Taurus."

"The bull," she cried, seizing the hauler by both shoulders. "Of course. It's obvious, isn't it?"

Gorp blushed. "This is my boy, Hubert," he said.

She eyeballed the youth. His arms were like string beans. "Hm. Must take after his mother."

"You don't know the half of it, Queen."

Salvo, who considered idle conversation a waste, took command of the situation. "Well. Much to be done. Carry on, men," he ordered.

Gorp and Hubert bowed to Queen Eridu, and she shimmered off. Hubert was happy to meet a real, live queen, but as he watched the Throne Bearers carry her off on their shoulders he couldn't help wondering why, if she was the most powerful person in Sumeria, she needed four guys to carry her around.

Later that morning Salvo, eager to get back to the Queen-manipulating game, accompanied her on a tour of the Ziggurat. "Your Majesty, these raids by the Assyrians are becoming more and more frequent. The time to act is now."

She pointed to a gap in a low stone wall. "That alcove over there. What's that going to be?"

Salvo consulted a blueprint. "That would be Your Majesty's . . . 'Garden of Peace and Freedom.'" His tone of voice suggested that he didn't care much for gardens, peace, or freedom.

"Splendid," she said. "Be sure to fill it with lots and lots of lilacs. They're so reassuring, don't you think?"

"Noted," replied the Prime Minister through clenched teeth, signaling her Throne Bearers to keep the tour moving along. "Now, as I was saying, the situation is critical. Our valley can only produce enough food for one people, not two. If we don't stop Ajax and his band of mountain savages from stealing our water and our crops, it will mean the end of us all."

Ajax was the leader of the Assyrians. The mere mention of his name struck fear in the heart of every Sumerian.

"They do seem to be at something of a disadvantage where water is concerned," she said thoughtfully.

"Your Majesty, if the gods wanted the Assyrians to have water, they would have made it run *up*hill," he countered solemnly.

As she was sorting this out, Salvo pressed on. "So, may I have Your Majesty's permission to marshal the forces for a devastating attack, and make the world safe for—'peace and freedom'?"

His eyes gleamed. Salvo was simply nuts about devastating attacks.

"Really, Salvo," she said calmly. "You should know that as a Libra, I never take the advice of a Capricorn when Venus is in retrograde."

FIVE

"Three turnips and a rutabaga?" Ajax's enraged voice echoed off the walls of the dark, torchlit cave deep in the Zagros Mountains.

"Three turnips and a rutabaga?" he repeated, causing the ringleader to cower closer to the floor. If he wanted to cower any deeper, he'd have to dig a trench.

"Well, Ajax, sir, we ran into a snag. Fellow named Gorp, kind of broad at the shoulder and narrow at the hip."

"I'm not interested in excuses," roared Ajax. "A mountain full of starving people, and all you have to offer is THREE TURNIPS AND A RUTABAGA?"

With a shark crack Ajax's whip lashed out and wrapped around the ringleader's neck. He could only squeak out a few words. "It *is* . . . a mighty fine . . . rutabaga, sir."

"Then I hope you enjoy it, because it's going to be YOUR LAST MEAL," Ajax bellowed. Two burly

guards stormed in and seized the ringleader by each arm. "Take him away!"

The guards did. This was the third ringleader in a month.

Halfway up the Ziggurat, poor Hodja was straining hard against the rope around his neck. The sledge carried a full load—four water jugs for the thirsty workers above—and though Hubert's sledge was considerably smaller than his father's, it was still a lot of weight for one onager to pull.

"There's gotta be a better way to do this," thought Hubert, walking alongside his friend.

"Hey, water boy. Pick up the pace," said a husky voice from behind. Hubert knew what was coming: another round of verbal torture—or worse—from the Punks, a trio of nasty teenagers who had been giving him grief for as long as he could remember. The husky voice belonged to Jiff, the rat-faced one.

"It's Baby Hubie," pitched in Cliff, the pimply one. In ten years of taunting, this was the highest level of repartee Cliff had managed to achieve. Dirk, the smelly one, brought up the rear. All three carried "adult" tools—pickaxes, shovels, sledgehammers—a fact of which they were extremely proud.

As the Punks passed, Jiff helped himself to a ladleful of water, took a sip, and dumped the rest over Hubert's head. In the stifling heat this didn't constitute much of an attack, but it was still degrading. Cliff upped the ante by seizing Hubert's shorts and giving him a ferocious wedgie, and Dirk yanked Hodja's tail. Hodja snapped at him.

"Ooh, the itty-bitty horsey almost bit me," said Dirk.

"He's not a horse. He's an onager," Hubert replied, adjusting his pants.

"Like I care."

"Leave us alone, okay? We're just doing our job."

"You call that a job?" sneered Jiff, brandishing his heavy pickax. "*This* is a job. Come on, men," he called to his pals, and all three clomped up the hill. Hodja bared his teeth and made another move toward

Dirk's retreating rump, but the rope choked him off in midlunge.

"Hodja, this system sucks," Hubert said as he loosened the knot. "If only we could shift the load to some other part of your body. . . ." He snapped his fingers. "That's it!"

Abandoning his duties, Hubert headed straight for the riverside, where he collected a few choice pieces of driftwood. Using every tool in his box (which he had luckily rescued from Gorp's closet just that morning), he cut, trimmed, and shaped them, then nailed them together into something resembling a narrow picture frame, which he fit over Hodja's shoulders. The onager was now sporting the world's first yoke.

"You're gonna love this," Hubert said as he attached a rope to each side. "See, it transfers the weight from your skinny little neck to your big, strong shoulders—which redirects the force vectors so that you can pull just as much weight with a whole lot less effort!"

Hodja gave the new invention an experimental tug. The sledge moved much more easily. He grasped the concept immediately and rewarded Hubert with a big slurp on the cheek. Someday Hubert would have to teach him a different way to show gratitude.

Returning to the work site, Hubert excitedly delivered the same explanation to his father, who was guiding Meg and Ed up a ramp with a full load of bricks. Having proven to himself that the yoke worked, Hubert had immediately built a bigger, stronger version that would fit a pair of oxen. Gorp listened patiently, and when his son was finished, he exploded.

"So that's what you've been up to! We've got guys up here about to keel over in the noonday sun, and you're off tinkering with some harebrained contraption? Sheesh!" Shaking his head, he continued up the hill, leaving Hubert holding the double yoke in his hands. Apparently, a demonstration would be required.

At noon the lunch bell rang, and Gorp and his best friend, Carl, retreated to a shady spot near the top of the Ziggurat, where they ate and discussed their favorite subject: the difficulty of raising adolescents.

"You gotta be patient, Gorp," said Carl between bites on a big joint of beef. "Maybe he'll grow out of it."

"I dunno. Sometimes I think he's—you know—a few bricks short of a load. Like the other day, I brought home a nice loaf of bread. The kid cuts it into slices."

Carl winced. Hoping to console his buddy, he offered the bone to Gorp, who always enjoyed gnawing on those last stubborn bits of gristle. "I feel for you, pal. But I'm tellin' ya, with daughters it's even worse."

Just then they were interrupted by a low rumble, which quickly became a low roar, which became a loud WHOOSHING sound as a fully loaded sledge came thundering down from the peak of the Ziggurat.

"Check it out," chuckled Gorp. "Some doofus let his rig get away from him."

"Hey, Gorp. That looks like *your* rig," Carl observed as it zoomed past. He was proven correct when Hubert appeared, racing after the accelerating sledge as fast as he could move. But it was hopeless. Panting to a stop, the best he could do was yell, "Look out below!"

All three watched in silence as the sledge continued along its path of destruction. Workers and animals scattered, mud bricks flew in all directions, ladders and scaffolding toppled like dominoes. Reaching the base of the Ziggurat, the sledge sailed into a quarry and smashed to smithereens.

Hubert felt his dad's eyes boring into the back of his head. He turned to face his executioner.

"I just wanted to demonstrate the yoke to you, Dad. I mean, you wouldn't listen to me earlier, so I thought . . . but when I went to put it on Meg and Ed, Ed got spooked—he spooks real easy, did you know that?—and he pushed the sledge over a little . . . cliff, and it . . . kind of got away from us. Me. Anyway, you've been talking about getting a new sledge, so it's really not that big a disaster. Right, Dad? Right?"

SIX

The next morning Gorp and Hubert saddled up Meg and Ed and rode off to buy a new sledge. Still pretty steamed, Gorp didn't really want to spend time around his son just now, but he figured it was safer than leaving him alone—who knew what kind of trouble he might get himself into? Hubert tried to make small talk along the way, but his dad kept his eyes locked on the road.

When they reached Big Al's New and Certified Pre-Owned Sledge Dealership, Al was out front doing a commercial. Since this was way before television, Al just gave his sales pitches to whoever happened to be within earshot. As a result, he had developed the loudest voice in the Tigris-Euphrates Valley, which is how he got the name Big Al. (It certainly didn't refer to his height, which was four feet nine inches in his thickest socks.)

"At Big Al's New and Certified Pre-Owned Sledge Dealership, Sumeria's number one transportation outlet, we've got the real deals. Whether you're hauling rocks or potatoes, warthogs or mother-in-laws—but I repeat myself—Big Al's got a sweet ride for you." He jumped up onto the fender of an economy sedan to deliver the wrap-up. "That's Big Al's, where our aim is to put you on the skids."

Scanning the crowd, Big Al's customer-seeking radar locked in on the burly gent who had just entered the lot and was kicking the runners of a used model near the showroom. Al was at Gorp's side in a heartbeat.

"An excellent choice, sir," he trumpeted. "I can tell you know quality when you see it. Low mileage, excellent maintenance record. Pampered by it sole owner, a widow who never drove it over two miles an hour." He leaned in and spoke out of the side of his oversized mouth. "But if you open her up, she'll do three."

"It's kind of small," said Gorp. "I need something for my hauling business."

Al smacked his forehead with the palm of his hand. "A professional! I should've known. Look, chief, I'm not gonna waste your time with these heaps. A man of your stature and discriminating taste deserves the very best. Follow me, if you will."

Gorp always considered himself his own man, but Al's slick salesmanship had thrown a fog across his mind. Almost before he knew it, he found himself in the showroom, where the pint-sized huckster positioned himself next to a large object draped in purple cloth.

"Presenting . . . direct from its mind-blowing

debut at the Lagash Transportation Expo . . . the Bronze Bomber." He whipped away the cloth with a flourish, and Gorp's eyes popped as he beheld the most beautiful sledge he had ever seen: big, sleek, and nearly glowing with a deep golden luster.

"Just got it in this morning. You'll be the first proud owner in the entire metropolis of Ur. Whaddaya think of that, Mister. . . . Sorry, I didn't catch your name."

"Gorp," said Gorp, running his hand along the smooth cargo bed. "How much?"

"We'll work with you, Gorp," said Big Al. "Uma, come on out here," he called toward the back, and out stepped an extraordinarily pretty girl of about Hubert's age. She glided directly toward the prospective customer, cool and confident, a chip off the old block.

"My daughter handles the finances—she'll take care of you. Now, if you'll excuse me, I've got a lot full of eager customers to satisfy. I leave you in capable hands." He patted Uma on the head. "Give 'im a great deal, honey." Then he added under his breath, "Not too great."

While Al went off to reel in another catch, Uma sidled over to Gorp, ignoring Hubert completely. "Magnificent, isn't it?" she gushed.

Gorp's nostrils flared as he took a deep whiff.

"I know," she purred. "You never quite get used to that new sledge smell, do you?"

That did it. Hubert's voice cut through the velvet sales spiel.

"Come on, Dad. This is exactly like your old one, but with a better paint job," he said.

Uma glared at the intruder, but Gorp was deaf to his son's objections, anyway. "It's so shiny," he said breathlessly.

"Eight coats of Harvest Gold lacquer," Uma said.

Hubert approached the sledge and examined a flimsy wicker grid lashed to the front. "What's this supposed to be?" he asked Uma, a bit sharply.

"Rhino bars," she fired back. "For protection."

"There are no rhinoceroses around here."

"See how well they work?"

"That's an old joke."

"Not yet it isn't," she countered drily.

Hubert's good manners told him it was rude to argue with someone he'd just met, and his good sense told him it was stupid to argue with an extraordinarily pretty girl of about his own age, but he couldn't stand to see anybody get ripped off, especially his dad. He stared her right in the eye.

"Look. You people sell the same lame products year in and year out, with no improvements. The only thing that's being perfected around here is your sales pitch."

Uma stayed calm. "Let me ask you something, uh . . ."

"Hubert."

"Catchy. Hubert, are you the buyer here or is your father?"

"Well, he is, but . . ."

"That's what I thought," she said curtly, and turned her attention back to Gorp, who was staring at the sledge's grillwork like a snake under the influence of a particularly charming mongoose. "Sir, you're obviously a man who knows his own mind. I'm sure you'd never allow your judgment to be clouded by the misguided notions of a callow youth. Even if he does happen to be your own son."

"Does it have cup holders?" Gorp asked.

She slowly reached across him and pressed a button on the dashboard, and an adorable double cup holder obligingly sprang into position.

"Where do I sign?" asked Gorp.

Uma shot Hubert a prim smile: checkmate. She was quite pleased with herself, having—as they say in the sales biz—"closed on a minor point."

On the way home, grinding and scraping their way along the deeply rutted road, Gorp happily turned to Hubert. "Smooth, huh?"

"Sure, Dad," he answered glumly.

Hubert sized up the situation. The new sledge was just as slow as the old one. The oxen were still tied to it by ropes around their horns. The only difference was a coat of cheap gold paint, which was already starting to blister and peel in the noonday sun.

It was time to get serious.

SEVEN

"It all comes down to friction," Hubert told Hodja as he pried out the nails that fastened the runners of his compact sledge to its frame. This required a hammer, which had meant another trip to the left side of the top shelf of Gorp's closet. He panicked for a moment when the box wasn't there, but was relieved to find it on the *right* side.

Gorp was taking it up a notch.

"If I can reduce the friction between the runners and the ground," Hubert continued, "maybe it'll reduce the friction between me and my dad."

Hodja looked dubious.

Once Hubert had the runners off, he replaced them with four wooden feet he'd made by sawing up the lid of his childhood toy box. The sledge looked like a turtle on tiptoe. The scheme didn't show much promise, but he had to start somewhere.

After attaching Hodja to the sledge by his yoke (at least the yoke was working okay), Hubert gave him the signal. The onager exerted a mighty pull, and the sledge immediately flipped over. Now it looked like a *dead* turtle. "Don't worry, boy, we're just getting started," Hubert said.

Every night after dinner, Hubert would disappear into his room to continue the process of trial and error. Mostly error.

First he mounted the sledge on four high stilts and walked behind it, operating the hind legs like levers. The contraption went about four steps before it collapsed in a heap.

Next he made four big bamboo springs and mounted the sledge on them, but this version was about as well-behaved as a bucking bronco.

Then there was the attempt at a flying version, which featured wings made from the living-room drapes. Hubert flapped them until his arms were ready to fall off, but the sledge didn't budge an inch. "Friction," he kept saying to Hodja. "We've got to eliminate the friction."

One Sunday morning Hodja made a suggestion. Retrieving the peel from Hubert's breakfast banana, he dropped it in his friend's lap.

"Yecch," Hubert said, but after Hodja gave him a don't-be-so-quick-to-dismiss-this look, Hubert got the point. He jumped to his feet. "You're right, Hodja. It's worth a try."

Hubert, Hodja, and Spike ate bananas until they were ready to pop, and Hubert carefully laid the peels out in front of the runners, like a carpet. He climbed aboard the sledge. "This might do it," said Hubert, just before his father arrived carrying an overfilled laundry basket.

"Hey, Hube, you forget? It's laundry daaaaaa-ayyy—"

Gorp's first unlucky step was directly onto the end of the banana trail. So was his second. So were the next twenty-three steps, which is how long Gorp danced along the slick path before he and the basket both became airborne. Gorp landed with an earthshaking thud, and the laundry floated down over him like confetti. A pair of boxer shorts were draped over his head.

Hubert skipped the explanation for once. "Laundry. Check. I'll get right on it," he said.

This was all, of course, well before Whirlpool, Maytag, and GE, let alone laundromats. You washed clothes by toting them down to the riverbank and bashing them against a rock until the dirt came out. On the desirability scale, Hubert ranked this chore somewhere between hauling water and clipping his dad's toenails.

There was one good thing about laundry day, though: the damp sand along the river made an excellent sketch pad. Using a stick, Hubert could lay out his designs on the smooth surface. If they didn't come out right, he would just erase them with a tree branch and start over.

When he and Hodja arrived at the river, it had been early morning. Now the sun was high in the sky and the laundry was still in the basket. He had, however, already made and erased over fifty drawings. Hodja nudged the basket toward his friend. Hubert nudged it right back. "In a minute," he said.

The sketch Hubert was working on a doozy: a one-quarter-scale rendering of Gorp's new Bronze Bomber, perfect in every detail, but without the runners. He'd been staring at it for a long while. He knew that something else, something friction-reducing, something revolutionary, should go between the sledge and the ground.

But what?

Hubert was stymied. His mother used to say that the best way to break up a mental logjam was to think about something else for a while. Looking for a diversion, Hubert plucked a daisy and twirled it in his fingers, admiring its shape and symmetry, then tossed it in the river. He played for a while with a family of pill bugs; but when they got tired of the game, they curled up into balls and rolled away.

"I'm not getting anywhere," thought Hubert as he bit into a round oatmeal cookie.

Finishing the cookie, he absentmindedly skipped a few flat stones across the flowing water. One, two, three, four, five skips . . . each skip created a series of spreading circular ripples. The yellow disk of the sun blazed overhead.

There were circles everywhere—except in Hubert's mind. "How do you eliminate friction?" he thought.

Meanwhile, Hodja had given up on his young master and was exploring the hillside above. He amused himself by sticking his inquisitive snout into a series of gopher holes; but when he hit an occupied one, the indignant resident gave him a bite on the nose. Startled, Hodja stumbled backward, lost his footing, and rolled down the hill, hoof over flank. He somersaulted right past Hubert, who was too deep in thought to notice, and plunged into the river.

Now Hodja was up to his neck in the Euphrates, and he'd never been much of a swimmer. Neighing and whinnying for help was of no use; Hubert was oblivious to his cries. "I'll just have to save myself," Hodja decided, "and when I do, I'm going to go live with somebody normal."

Luckily, Hodja spotted a big log floating downstream and, with a lot of huffing and puffing, managed to clamber up on top of it. But when the log started to rotate, he had to scramble frantically to stay on board.

Back on the bank, Hubert had all but abandoned his project. If a solution to the friction problem hadn't come to him yet, maybe it never would. He'd just have to round up Hodja and—by the way, where was Hodja?

Looking up from his drawing, he was greeted by

the highly unusual sight of his pet onager in midriver, logrolling like a prizewinning lumberjack.

An epiphany is when you experience a sudden realization or perception of reality. Hubert had had a few epiphanies, such as the time he realized his father would never understand the difference between inventing and goofing off. But the epiphany he had when he saw the log revolving beneath Hodja's hooves, nearly frictionless, was the epiphany to beat all epiphanies.

Unaware of his best friend's fight for survival, Hubert completed his drawing by adding a circle beneath each of the sledge's four corners. "That's it, Hodja! We did it! You're a genius," he cried.

"Fine," thought Hodja, "now get out here and rescue me." But Hodja would have to sort this one out for himself, since Hubert was already sprinting home to build the world's first wheel.

EIGHT

The hard part—conception—was over. The easy part—implementation—went quickly.

Hubert used every tool in the box. With his hammer he fastened three long wooden planks together, edge to edge, with bronze straps. With his saw he cut out four disks, each about two feet in diameter. After smoothing them with his file, he fastened them to the ends of two axles made of poplar trunks.

Hodja, having survived his ordeal at the river, returned in the middle of all this activity. He was grumpy and wet, but he soon got caught up in Hubert's enthusiasm. "This time it's gonna work, Hodja," Hubert said as he attached the axles to the bottom of his upside-down sledge. Now it was ready for the all-important testing phase.

Together they righted the modified sledge. Hubert put his hand against it and solemnly turned to his friend. "This is a small push for a boy, Hodja, but one giant shove for mankind."

They held their breath, and Hubert gave the new-fangled vehicle a push.

It rolled.

And not just an inch or two; it traveled several feet before coasting to a graceful stop. Hodja's jaw dropped. Hubert gave a wild whoop of delight. "Wait till we show Dad!" he said.

Gorp had spent most of the afternoon at Carl's house, chewing the fat. Not conversing—it was an actual lump of suet. As he strolled home he opened his wallet and took out a portrait of himself with Samarra and Hubert, then age two. The picture made his pants sag a little (it was chiseled on a stone tablet), but he carried it anyway because it reminded him of happier times.

Gorp had been head over heels in love with his wife. He was amazed at how effortlessly she could create something new out of ordinary, everyday stuff—especially in the kitchen. For example, she was the first person to combine vegetables, meat, spices, and hot water into a tasty concoction she called "soup." This led to another invention, the spoon, which eliminated the slurping sounds Gorp made when he fed straight from the bowl. The fork soon followed, preventing many a bitten finger.

Another creation of Samarra's made it much easier for them to get a good night's sleep: gravel-filled pillows. (Up until then, they had used solid stone blocks.)

What a woman!

Gorp put the picture back in his wallet as he approached the house. "Those were the days," he said to himself. The days before the tragic umbrella mishap, before he started hating inventions, before Hubert started destroying things—such as his new Bronze Bomber, which his son had upended in the driveway and was apparently dismantling with a crowbar.

"Dad, your troubles are over," Hubert announced as he pried off one of the runners.

"What on earth are you doing?" gasped Gorp.

"This is it! This is what I've been working toward, and I finally got it—"

"'Cause I'm telling you right now, if you've done anything to void the warranty—"

"Don't worry about that," Hubert said as he went to work on the second runner. "This is going to change your life. Please, Dad, trust me. Just this once."

Before long, Hubert had the Bomber back in one piece and Hodja was in his harness. The only difference was, the device now rode on the four new wheels instead of the two old runners.

"Get in, Dad," Hubert said.

"I don't like the look of this. Not one bit."

"Trust me."

Gorp gingerly climbed in next to his son. "You don't mean to tell me that your puny little onager is gonna move my big, beautiful sledge."

"Technically, Dad, it's not a sledge anymore. I call it a cart." Gorp just stared at him. Hubert handed him the reins. "Go ahead."

Gorp decided to humor him—what could it hurt? He gave the reins a shake and was shocked when the cart began to move. He jumped off.

"How'd you do that?" asked Gorp.

"It's the round things, Dad," Hubert said. "I call 'em wheels. Cool, huh?"

Gorp chewed his lip for a moment, then got back into the driver's seat.

"I don't know, son. It doesn't seem . . . natural."

"Maybe not," Hubert said as the cart started to move again, "but you've gotta admit, it's smooth." Hodja didn't appear to be working at all. In fact, he was almost prancing. "What's more, I think these wheel things could be used all sorts of ways. I've got tons more ideas—"

"Son, I think we're picking up speed here—" Gorp pointed out.

"Yeah, we're really rolling now! Maybe because we're on a little hill . . ."

"So, how do you stop it?"

"Stop?"

"Yeah, stop."

"Oh, that's easy," said Hubert. "Hodja, stop."

Hodja halted on a dime (those obedience classes had definitely paid off), but the cart was really barreling along now. When it overtook the onager, the fender scooped him up like a cowcatcher, and he found himself sitting between father and son, wearing the yoke like a necklace.

Hubert snapped his fingers. "Brakes. I forgot brakes." Hodja and Gorp exchanged a look of sheer horror.

Now careening out of control, the cart left the roadbed and started bouncing down a steep, grassy hill. It was rolling much too fast for the trio to jump off.

"Hubert, if we live through this, I'm gonna kill you," Gorp said.

Now moving faster than even the fastest horse could gallop, the cart was headed straight for a huge ficus tree. Hodja covered his eyes with his hooves.

Hubert searched his mind for a solution, without success. It was up to Gorp to save the day.

Swinging into action, the big fella handed the reins to his son and clambered toward the back of the wildly bucking cart. Holding fast to the tailgate with both hands, he jumped out and planted his bare heels into the ground, digging two deep furrows in the soft earth. The cart began to slow.

"Can you steer it away from the tree?" Gorp yelled, his teeth chattering from the bumpy ride.

"What do you mean by 'steer'?" Hubert asked.

"Can you change direction?"

"No, but that's another great idea, Dad!" He'd have to make a note of it—if they happened to survive the impact.

But Gorp was known throughout Mesopotamia for his powerful legs, and with a mighty effort he managed to bring the massive cart and its occupants to a halt within inches of plowing into the tree.

His face now the color of heavy storm clouds, Gorp slowly made his way around to the front of the cart, wrenched one of the wheels loose from the Bronze Bomber, and flung it a hundred yards.

"Okay, I get your point," Hubert said, fearful that he might be Gorp's next projectile. "Don't give it another thought. I'll get rid of the wheels. That's a promise. Consider it done."

NINE

A cross from the Ziggurat was a broad public square that served as a gathering place, a parade ground, and, on Tuesdays and Saturdays, an open-air market. Beneath canvas awnings, vendors and farmers peddled everything from cookpots to artwork to fruit to sandals to monkeys.

Hubert was squatting against one of the buildings bordering the square, next to the four wheels he had made. He had promised to get rid of the cursed things, but he couldn't bring himself to just throw them out. Maybe somebody else who appreciated their value would buy them and put them to good use.

But Hubert had been at the marketplace since dawn, and so far all he had to show for it was a sunburn. He had started the day asking ten shekels per wheel, then five, then two wheels for three shekels, then two for one. He was considering offering them up as "free to good home" when a couple with two small children strolled past.

"Excuse me, sir," Hubert began, "I don't suppose you'd like to buy these. No reasonable offer refused."

"What are they for?" asked the father.

"I'll show you." Hubert picked up one of the wheels and rolled it toward him. Never having seen a wheel before, let alone one in motion, the family jumped back in fear. Losing momentum, it tipped over and rattled to a stop on the cobblestones.

One of the kids moved toward it with interest, but her mother snatched her back. "Don't touch it, Mary," she warned, "it might still be alive."

"They're not dangerous," Hubert protested, but the family was already hustling off. "Really! All they do is reduce"—he continued, but found he was just talking to himself—"friction."

The afternoon dragged on. And on and on and on. Hubert must have nodded off in the hot sun because the next thing he knew, someone was standing over him, holding one of the wheels in the air.

"This is cute," she said. "What are you asking for it?"

He recognized her right away as Uma, daughter of Big Al the Sledge Dealer. He had no energy left to haggle, least of all with a professional.

"Nothing," he said dejectedly. "You can have it."

Uma pursed her lips in disapproval. "Excuse me, isn't this a marketplace? Where people buy, sell, barter—"

"That's not my specialty. I'm an inventor." He corrected himself. "Was. I guess I'm a hauler."

She continued to examine the merchandise. Whatever it was, it was certainly well made. "Ahh, *now* I remember. Hubert. The guy who tried to bust my chops the other day. You nearly cost me a sweet commission."

"I was just looking out for my dad."

"Right," Uma said, peering through the axle hole. "So what are these things, anyway?"

"They're called wheels. I invented them."

"What do they do?"

"Make sledges go faster."

"Anything else?"

"Yeah. They make your father yell at you."

"Very interesting," she said, rotating it in her hands.

"I thought if I impressed him, he'd let me be an inventor. But it didn't work out. So I figured I'd just try to sell them."

"What, with no business plan? No product launch?"

"I don't want to launch anything. I just want to unload them."

"Well, you still need some sales technique," she scolded. "Here, watch a pro."

In no time flat Uma had snagged a passing couple carrying an infant. "Now, here's an attractive young pair," she began. "And what a beautiful baby! Coochie coochie coo." She tickled junior under the chin.

"I'll bet you folks are just starting out," Uma went on. "Feathering your nest, am I right?" The young father nodded. "Knew it. I've got something here. . . .

I've been waiting all afternoon for someone to come along who could really appreciate it."

She held the wheel up like a trophy. "Take a look at this. Have you ever seen anything like it? The graceful curves. The solid feel. And what workmanship. Just run your hand over that finish."

"Ooh," said the wife as Uma handed it to her.

"What is it?" said the husband.

"What do you think it is?" asked Uma with an enigmatic smile.

"Coffee table?"

Uma turned to Hubert. "What an eye. Did I tell you, Hubie? These two weren't born yesterday."

"Now, wait just a minute," Hubert protested, but she silenced him with a ferocious glare.

Now the husband was inspecting the artifact.

"Aren't coffee tables supposed to have legs?" he asked.

"Legs sold separately," she fired back, picking up one of the axles.

"All right, that's enough," Hubert growled, taking it from her.

"What's your partner so upset about?" asked the wife. "We'll pay for the legs."

"They're not legs, they're axles," said Hubert, his voice rising. "And she's not my partner, she's my . . . she's not my anything."

Hubert wrestled the wheel out of the husband's hands.

"I'll give you five shekels if you throw in the legs," the husband said. They didn't really need a coffee table, but everybody loves a bargain.

"NO SALE!" said Hubert with finality.

The family started to walk away, muttering indignantly. Uma followed, desperate to salvage the deal. "I have to apologize for my associate. You know how these creative types can be." But it was too late.

Uma marched back to Hubert, who was standing with an axle in one hand and a wheel in the other.

"Quite the little deal-killer, aren't you?"

"Coffee tables. Is that your idea of salesmanship? Lying to people?"

"You call it lying. I call it giving the customers what they want. Besides, you were the one who said you wanted to unload this junk. Why should you care how I do it?"

"I changed my mind. I'm not going to let you foist my invention on some poor saps who are just going to end up bumping their shins on it."

"See if I ever help you again," she snapped, turning to go just as Big Al arrived, toting a shopping bag and chomping on a pomegranate.

"There you are, kiddo. Ready to go?"

"Sure, Pop," she said.

Al recognized Hubert from his lot the other day and flashed him a solicitous smile. "Hey, kid. How's your old man doing with his heavy-duty cutie?"

"*He* likes it."

"Glad to hear it. What's that you're holding there?"

"Hubert says he came up with something that makes sledges move faster."

"Oh, you have, have you?" Al said. "Let's take a look."

Hubert was in no mood to give a demonstration, but he didn't want to be rude. He reattached a wheel to each end of the axle and handed it to the diminutive dealer. "This is just a prototype, of course."

"That's a big word for such a little kid."

"It means original model, trial version—"

"I know what a prototype is, pip-squeak." Big Al held the wheels and axle over his head like a barbell. "Hey, look how strong I am."

Hubert tried to stay calm. "They go underneath the sledge. To eliminate friction."

"Yeah. Uh-huh. Good luck, chum," Al responded with a condescending chuckle. He dropped the wheels and axle at Hubert's feet with a clunk.

Hubert might have let it go at that, but now his pride was at stake. There's only so much abuse a guy can take in one day. "I've tried them," he said, setting his jaw. "They work great."

"Look, junior. Sledge technology's been around a gazillion years. If there was a way to improve on it—"

"I *have* improved on it," Hubert said, holding up one of the wheels. "Take a long, hard look, mister.

'Cause one day these are going to put you out of business."

Al had never backed down from a challenge in his life, and he wasn't about to start. He took a step toward Hubert. "Is that a threat or a promise?"

Hubert took a step toward Al. "It's a fact."

"Ooh. Tough guy." They were nose to nose. Uma stepped between them.

"Why don't you two resolve this like civilized people," she suggested.

"What's that supposed to mean?" asked Big Al.

"We'll have a contest," she said.

They both turned to her. "A contest?" they asked simultaneously.

Uma's face broke into a grin. Her life had been a little dull lately, and this was sure to spice it up.

"Just leave the details to me," she said.

TEN

L ike most cities in the years before newspapers, magazines, radio, television, or the Internet, Ur had a town crier. This was not, as you might think, a person who was impossible to cheer up, but rather a large man with a deep, impressive voice whose job was to walk up and down the streets hollering out news and public announcements. For three days before the Great Race (as it would later come to be known), the Town Crier's speech went like this:

"Sunday, Sunday, Sunday! Don't miss the white-knuckle action at Mesopotamia Speedway, where you'll see two proud competitors locked in a head-to-head, no-holds-barred fight to the finish line. It's youth versus experience. It's technology versus brute force. It's—and here's a first—ox versus onager! What will be the outcome? Will it be muscle over mind, or brains over bronze? You'll find out at Mesopotamia Speedway, where the wood hits the dirt. That's Sunday, Sunday, Sunday! Be there."

It was now Sunday, the day of reckoning, and the entire town had turned out for the big event. The viewing stands along a fifty-yard stretch of Main Street were filled to capacity, and concessionaires worked the crowd, selling peanuts, fruit, and beets-on-a-stick.

Jiff, Cliff, and Dirk moved through the throng taking bets. Betting was outlawed in Ur, but people did it anyway. The Punks were offering seventeen-to-one odds against Hubert.

Queen Eridu, seated on a purple throne on the Royal Reviewing Stand, signaled the Royal Sportscasters, Bob and Terry, to commence the Royal Play-by-Play and Color. They took their positions at the megaphones.

"Well, Bob, you couldn't ask for a more perfect racing day," Terry began peppily.

"That's right, Terry," Bob chimed in, "and what an unusual event this promises to be. We've been hearing a lot about this youngster and his highly unconventional—what does he call that thing again?"

"It's a Carrier Atop Round Things, Bob, or CART for short."

"Fascinating, Terry. Now, tell us a little more about today's matchup."

The Queen loved listening to the Royal Sportscasters, especially when they used snazzy expressions

like "they came to play," "that is one highly motivated individual," and "what a change in momentum."

"Each driver will be pulling two thousand pounds of bricks, and I understand these payloads were weighed and measured under the supervision of Prime Minister Salvo himself."

Down at the starting line Hubert nervously watched the bricks being loaded onto his little cart.

Its axles were bending, and for a heart-stopping moment he was sure they'd break. But when the last brick was added to the pile, the axles held.

Sitting next to Hubert's cart was Big Al's industrial-strength hauler, yoked to his two strongest oxen. Al had been working the animals out all week, giving them pep talks and feeding them high-protein alfalfa. They looked well rested and confident.

The race wouldn't start for a few minutes, so Hubert went off to find his dad, hoping for a few words of advice or encouragement. He located Gorp high in the stands, sitting with Carl. "Thanks for being here, Dad. It means a lot to me."

Gorp searched for an appropriate response. His feelings were, to say the least, mixed. On one hand, he didn't want his son exposed to ridicule. On the other hand, he desperately wanted Hubert to give up this creativity nonsense, and maybe a stinging public defeat would convince the kid to quit once and for all. Back on the first hand, the family reputation was on the line, and a loss would expose Gorp to ridicule as well. Back on the second hand, he had bet a week's pay on Big Al.

Gorp decided to play it down the middle. "Just give it all you got, son."

This wasn't what Hubert was hoping for, but it was something. He snapped his dad a salute and headed down to the track.

What Hubert didn't know was, while he was up in the stands Big Al had been having himself a closer look at his competitor's ridiculous-looking cart. Surely it would be no match for his superhauler and bulked-up oxen. But something about the design made him just the faintest bit nervous. A sneaky idea crept into his head.

At exactly noon Queen Eridu made a brief welcoming speech and declared that the Great Race should get underway immediately. After all, she didn't want to be late for her palm reading. Everyone's attention turned to the starting line, where the two competitors waited for Uma to wave the green flag.

Big Al glanced down from the high seat of his mighty sledge. "I'll be waiting for you at the finish line, chump. If you make it that far." Hubert just wrapped the reins around his skinny wrists and gritted his teeth.

Suddenly Uma was waving the flag, the crowd was roaring, and Hubert was giving Hodja's reins a shake and yelling "Hyeahh," which was drowned out by Big Al's deafening "HYEAHHHH," and the race was on.

Hubert had done the math a dozen times. Taking into account the strength of two oxen, the size of one onager, the friction of a sledge, the grittiness of the dirt, and the efficiency of the wheel, he calculated that his two-thousand-pound brick load would cross the finish line 9.3 seconds ahead of Al's. But he had left out the most crucial factor: the sneakiness of a used sledge dealer. Big Al had swiped the pin that connected the cart to the yoke. So when Hodja took off toward the finish line, Hubert came with him . . . but the cart didn't.

Hubert was now bouncing along the ground on his stomach with a mouthful of gravel, unable to free his hands from the leather reins or to get the attention of his unstoppable onager. His cart hadn't moved an inch. Meanwhile, Al and his muscular oxen were making slow but steady progress toward the finish.

"Stop, Hodja," Hubert yelled. "Halt! Whoa! Cease! Desist! Cut it out! Ixnay!" But the onager just kept running. Hodja had been in training, too, and had learned all too well the lesson of focusing on a goal. "I *am* the finish line. I *am* the finish line," he told himself.

Finally Hubert got himself free of the reins, skidded to a stop on his belly, and sat up to clear his head just as Big Al came lumbering past in a cloud of dust. To add insult to injury, Al made a point of showing him the pin he'd stolen. "Sucker," he sneered.

The crowd roared as Al passed Hubert. Salvo narrowed his already narrow eyes. Gorp dug his nails into Carl's forearm. The Queen fanned herself with a palm leaf.

Hodja crossed the finish line and did a manic endzone dance, unaware that his load of bricks was sitting back at the start. Hubert was still on the ground. But the gloating expression on Big Al's goofy face spurred him to action. He sprinted back to the cart, grabbed the bumper, and pulled as hard as he could.

It didn't budge. A wave of derisive laughter rippled through the crowd.

He pulled again. And again. And again.

And then it budged.

The spectators gasped in unison, then fell silent. No one in the entire history of civilization had ever seen one person, let alone a fairly scrawny fifteen-year-old, budge a load of bricks that big. And now he wasn't just budging them, he was actually moving them, and now he was walking, and now he was walking pretty fast, and now he was running.

Gorp rubbed his eyes in disbelief. The crowd rose to its feet. "Go, Hubert," somebody yelled, and soon the whole stadium was cheering him on.

Up on the viewing stand, the Royal Sportscasters were working themselves into a frenzy. "That is one scrappy little Sumerian," Terry said.

Now only ten yards from the finish line, Big Al sensed the change in the air and looked over his shoulder to see Hubert coming up fast on his left flank. He whipped his oxen and called them names that can't be repeated here. The animals doubled their efforts, and then redoubled them, but Hubert was still gaining.

There was, of course, no such thing as a photo finish back then, but the Royal Artist was on hand to draw a sketch of what everybody saw: Hubert, eyes bulging and muscles straining, winning the race by a nose.

The scene at the finish line was megabedlam. Everybody mobbed the man of the hour. Hubert caught up with Hodja, who had by now recognized his error and was hanging his head in embarrassment. Quick to forgive, Hubert threw his arms around the beast's neck and gave him some victory noogies.

Bob and Terry pushed their way through the joyous crowd to the victor's side for the traditional post-race interview. "We're up close and personal with Hubert," Terry began, "the remarkable young fellow who has just defeated a much stronger competitor to become the new champion of short-distance hauling."

"This is competition at its finest," added Bob.

"A red-letter day."

"History in the making."

"It's certainly one for the books."

"What's a book?"

"I don't know, Bob, that just popped into my head."

Bob clamped his arm around Sumeria's newest celebrity. "Tell us, Hubert, how do you feel at this very moment?" But before he could answer, Uma appeared, grabbed the new champion of short-distance hauling by both shoulders, and gave him a big kiss. Right on the mouth.

"Ooooh," said the crowd.

"Nice," said Terry.

"Hubba–hubba," said Bob.

"Keep your slimy lips off my daughter, you under-handed overachiever," said Big Al, yanking her away.

"You're just being a sore loser," said Uma.

"Be that as it may," Al countered, then turned back to give Hubert another glare. "You're history, buster. You'll never see my daughter again."

Hubert would have liked to continue this dis-cussion—he had suddenly developed a whole new appreciation for the opposite sex—but just then his fans hoisted him to their shoulders and carried him off, shouting and singing at the top of their lungs. He soon lost sight of Uma, Big Al, and Hodja, and was only aware of the boiling mass of humanity be-neath him. He had become something he never in-tended to be: a hero. And he had to admit, it felt pretty good.

ELEVEN

That night Uma served her father his dinner in complete silence. He was mad at her, and she was mad at him, so they just clammed up. Big Al secretly enjoyed this, as it gave him a good long time to sulk over his crushing defeat, but by dessert he'd had his fill of both food and sulking. Wiping a few crumbs of date pie from his mouth, he said, "We've really got our work cut out for us now, kiddo."

"Doing what?" she replied icily.

"'Doing what?' I've got a whole fleet of sledges down at the lot waiting to be retrofitted."

She narrowed her eyes. "Oh. So now you're going into the wheel business. What a hypocrite."

Al knew better than to contradict her. "Hey. If you can't beat 'em, join 'em," he said.

Things were pretty quiet over at Hubert's house, too. Naturally, Gorp was proud of his boy for winning the Great Race, but he couldn't help worrying about what lay ahead for them both. After today you didn't have to be psychic to know that big changes were coming, and Gorp liked the word "change" about as much as he liked the word "invention."

Hubert went to bed early because tomorrow was going to be a big day: He'd been summoned to the palace by the Queen. The closest he'd ever come to entering the palace was when he and Gorp once delivered a load of mud to the front gate for the Queen's Royal Mud Bath. "I don't get it," Hubert had said to his father. "Everybody else takes baths to get mud *off*."

"It must be a Queen thing," Gorp had said.

Like everything else about her, Queen Eridu's throne room was done up in grand style. The ornate, high-backed throne stood at one end of a great arched hall with tall windows on each side. Colorful banners hung from the ceiling, each depicting a different sign of the zodiac. Stars and moons were painted all over the walls, and there were numerous life-sized marble statues of the Queen herself, striking various poses and wearing fanciful hats.

Queen Eridu had her faults, but you couldn't accuse her of excessive modesty.

Prime Minister Salvo escorted Hubert along the corridor toward the throne, their footsteps echoing off the stone walls. The Queen loved those walls for the booming, regal effect they gave to such pronouncements as "It is so decreed" and "We are not amused."

Salvo presented Hubert to the Queen with a bow, turned and bowed to Hubert, then threw in a few extra bows for good measure before withdrawing to skulk. (Skulking, which combines hiding, sneaking, spying, and plotting, is an activity much beloved by evil prime ministers. Salvo did so much skulking that the Queen had provided a special skulking area for him in a dark corner to the rear of the throne.)

"Hi, Queen," said Hubert with a smile.

This was a rather cheeky way to address a monarch, but she found his directness refreshing. "That was quite an impressive display yesterday, young man. Tell me," she said, beckoning him closer, "how did you do it? Was it sorcery?"

"No, Your Highness. I—"

"Witchcraft, then? Are you in league with the Devil?"

"No!"

"Perhaps you possess superhuman strength," she suggested. "Do you work out regularly?"

"Clearly not, Your Majesty," Salvo chipped in from his dark corner.

Hubert ignored the dig. "It's like I keep telling everybody, Queen, there's nothing magic about wheels. They just seem weird because they're new. It's simple science. Anybody could have invented them. I just happened to do it first."

"Hmm," the Queen said. This was at odds with her worldview, which ran more to fate, omens, harbingers, magic spells, and the like.

Salvo emerged from the shadows. "I can confirm that, Your Majesty. I've examined the device myself, and the principles involved appear to be quite sound." He lowered his voice. "In fact, I believe there may be applications of the wheel that could greatly benefit our society."

"Me, too!" said Hubert. "Almost anything you want to push or pull or lift—it's easier with a wheel. I've got tons of ideas—"

"As do I," Salvo interjected, gently taking the Queen's arm and escorting her down the steps from her throne. "As Your Majesty knows, Ajax's threat grows ever more serious." He guided her to one of the north-facing windows, where they looked out upon the distant Zagros Mountains, their cliffs dotted with spooky-looking caves. "With the proper modifications, this boy's little invention could give us just the military edge we ned to vanquish the Assyrians."

"Hmm," she said. "Hold that thought. Hubert, would it be possible, do you think, to create a horizontal wheel so large that people could hop aboard and ride round and round? Or perhaps a vertical one with little baskets, so they could go high in the air?"

Salvo rolled his eyes.

"Wow, are you ahead of the curve," Hubert said to the Queen, delighted by her ideas.

"You're too kind," she said. Salvo cleared his throat. "I'm sorry, Salvo. You were saying."

"Yes, Your Majesty." He took her arm again. "In order to ensure our national security—"

But Hubert was on a roll now. "You know where the wheel could really rock? The Ziggurat!"

"Hmm. Intriguing," she said as Hubert took her other elbow and led her across the room to the *south*-facing window, through which the construction site could be seen.

"I bet we could finish it up in no time flat," Hubert exclaimed. "Wouldn't that be cool?"

"Capital idea. Of course, the Ziggurat is the Prime Minister's department, not mine. I'm sure he'll be happy to be of assistance. Won't you, Salvo?"

"Pardon me, Your Majesty," Salvo said, "I didn't quite catch the gist of that."

"Well, you certainly can't expect this young man to oversee such a vast project all by himself. He'll need a helper of some kind."

Salvo was still hoping he'd misunderstood. "And that would be . . ."

"That would be you, dear boy."

The Prime Minister bared his teeth in an odd grimace.

"Salvo? What are you doing?"

"Smiling, Your Majesty," he answered.

"Oh. How nice." Queen Eridu clapped her hands twice, which is how monarchs often signal the end of a meeting. "Well, I must away. Time to have my tea leaves read. Salvo, show your new boss the way out," she commanded, and flounced off.

Hubert turned to the Prime Minister, beaming with enthusiasm. "So, looks like you and I'll be spending a lot of time together, huh?"

TWELVE

Just as Hubert had predicted, the Ziggurat went up a lot faster once the wheel was put in use. Wagons and carts delivered building materials three times as fast with a third of the effort. With the aid of log rollers, a few workers could push a massive stone block up a ramp. Ropes and pulleys lifted lumber and bricks to the top of walls in a fraction of the time it used to take. Wheelbarrows allowed one man to carry the load of four.

Practically overnight Hubert went from being one of the most ignored citizens of Sumeria to one of the most in-demand. The Queen named him Royal Technologist, and every day a line of foremen and project managers formed outside the construction tent, all waiting their turn to ask his advice on something or another.

Salvo's life changed dramatically, too. He used to have constant access to the Queen; now she seemed to have lost interest in him, preferring to spend her time either consulting with Hubert or playing with the new toy that was sweeping the nation: the yo-yo.

Salvo's duties at the Ziggurat were considerably less prestigious, too. It often fell to him to notify Hubert when the lunch wagon arrived or, worse, fetch him his falafel and hummus.

Another person who found himself outside Hubert's new circle of happiness was his father. Alone among the haulers, Gorp refused to abandon his trusty sledge. He figured that if dragging things along the ground was good enough for his father, and his father's father, it was sure as heck good enough for him. The only way he managed to stay employed was to work twice as hard as everyone else.

While Hubert was walking the site one afternoon

on a quality check, he came upon his dad plodding along a construction road with a load of logs.

"Hey, Dad, how's it going?" Hubert asked.

"I got no complaints," Gorp muttered.

"So. Still sticking with the Bronze Bomber, huh?"

"I paid good shekels for it, didn't I?"

"I see you switched over to the yoke I made, though."

"Had to. I guess Meg and Ed got jealous of the other oxen." He raised his shirt. "Meg gored me a couple of times."

"That's rough."

"It'll heal."

They walked along in silence for a while. Finally Hubert just blurted out what he was thinking. "Dad, you can't fight progress. Everybody else is adjusting. Why don't you?"

"Progress comes at a price," Gorp said. "I paid it once. I don't want to pay it again."

"But this time it's different," Hubert protested. "The wheel is a win-win situation. What do you think's gonna go wrong?"

"I don't know. But it'll be bad."

"What do you mean, 'bad'? Bad how?"

"I've got work to do," Gorp said, closing the subject.

Hubert's relationship with Uma wasn't exactly rip-
ping along, either. Big Al, a world-class grudge
bearer, was sticking to his anti-Hubert stance.

"But he did you a favor," she pointed out to her
father one day while they were bolting new wheels
onto old sledges. "Your business has tripled. Plus, he
never snitched on you for sabotaging his cart. I don't
see what you could possibly have against him."

"Someday you'll grow up and have children of
your own, and you can be inconsistent, hypocritical,
and unfair to *them*."

"Great," she said. "That makes me feel so much
better."

THIRTEEN

Miles away, high in the Zagros Mountains of Assyria, Ajax peered down at the city of Ur. Even from this distance, the Ziggurat was clearly visible, and getting more visible every day.

"They're up to something," Ajax said to his second-in-command, Colonel Karp. "Something evil."

"Absolutely," said the Colonel, whom Ajax had chosen for the job not for his soldiering ability but for his tendency to agree with everything Ajax said. He did, however, have a habit of asking annoying questions, such as "Why is the word 'colonel' pronounced 'kernel'?" (The reason was that Ajax wanted it pronounced that way, and disobeying the leader carried with it the distinct possibility of being crushed.)

"How do you know it's evil?" asked Colonel Karp.

"Because Sumerians are building it, and Sumerians are evil. Therefore, it must be evil, whatever it is."

"And why are the Sumerians evil? I'm sorry, I forget sometimes. Please don't crush me."

"Because they hog all the food, land, and water, leaving us stuck up here in these ridiculous caves. Any more questions?"

Colonel Karp sneaked a peak at the whip that Ajax always kept coiled on a special hook on his belt and decided to save any further questions for another day. "Whatever that thing is, it's going up pretty fast," he observed.

"One thing's for sure, Karp. They're going to use it to mount an attack."

"No question," he answered. "How do you think they're gonna get it up here?"

Ajax put his hand on his whip. "Get away from me, Karp," he growled.

Karp scurried off, leaving his boss gazing at the mysterious structure. What the devil were those people up to?

FOURTEEN

The wheel wasn't just changing life at the Ziggurat; it was changing life all over Sumeria.

As Royal Technologist, Hubert spent most
of his time cooking up new ways to use wheels. The
Queen even gave him a small staff to build and test
his prototypes, and the successful ones quickly found
their way into public use. Many of the more creative
citizens started building their own rolling vehicles,
and they spread like wildfire.

Wheel technology proved to be quite versatile.
During a single trip through downtown Ur, a passerby
might see a hand truck, a vegetable cart, a father pulling his little girl in a red wagon, an artisan making a
pot on a foot-driven pottery wheel, a baker flattening
dough with a rolling pin, a chef slicing pizza with a
pizza cutter, a baby in a stroller, a kid wearing a
beanie cap with a propeller on top, and a shopping cart
with—wouldn't you know it—one wobbly wheel.

For the first time in his life, Hubert felt that he
was making a difference in the world. He just wished
his dad could be proud of him. And that his mother

were around to share in his success. And that he could see Uma.

On the outskirts of town one morning, Farmer Omar was sitting at a crossroads on his new hay wagon, whistling a happy tune. It had been months since the last Assyrian raid, and he'd managed to harvest his entire crop of hay. Now he was on his way into town to sell it at the marketplace. "What a huge improvement this wagon is over my old hay sledge," he thought as he signaled for a left turn onto the main road, and pulled out.

But he had to hit the brakes (all wheeled vehicles by now included brakes) when a smaller, speedier cart came zipping past. It was moving so fast that the wind blew Omar's hat off.

"That was rude," Omar remarked to his horse as he climbed down to retrieve his hat—a dandy straw one with a wide brim that Gert had woven him as a wedding present. But before he could pick it up, another cart, moving even faster than the first, came screaming by from the other direction, flattening his hat into the dirt.

Omar jumped into the street, screaming and shaking his fist after the departing driver.

Road rage had come to Mesopotamia.

Other incidents followed quickly. When Omar was halfway to town, dozens of other vehicles were piling up behind his slow, overloaded hay wagon, and their drivers were hopping mad. Omar, who was a nice guy, would normally have pulled over to let them pass, but he was still miffed about his hat. Besides, some people turn into absolute beasts whenever they get in control of any kind of vehicle. "I may be slow," he thought as he clip-clopped along, "but I'm ahead of them."

Progress was taking a toll on the business district, too. The town square, which used to be a pleasant, peaceful gathering place for all the citizens of Ur, had turned into a hellish demolition derby, where wheeled vehicles of all sizes and shapes dashed about willy-nilly, pulled by oxen, horses, onagers, and even teams of speedy dogs. Pedestrians, who once took leisurely strolls through the square, stopping to chat with their fellow Urians, suddenly found themselves an endangered species. Every few minutes someone would yelp and jump up on a park bench or into somebody's shopwindow to avoid being squashed by an out-of-control cart.

Even worse, the ever-increasing traffic had to flow into and out of the central city along one main street, and the resulting bottleneck led to a lot of hot tempers and harsh words. It also created the world's first pothole, and at precisely nine minutes after noon, Farmer Omar drove his bursting-at-the-seams hay wagon right into it. The jolt snapped off the bottom third of his left front wheel, resulting in the world's first flat tire.

The hay spilled off the cart, spooking the horses. The horses reared back, scaring the oxen. The oxen

bellowed, scaring the other drivers. Everyone hit the brakes, and with a sickening, wrenching CRUNCH, everybody crashed into everybody else at the same time. Nobody outside the city could get in, and nobody inside the city could get out.

It was total gridlock.

FIFTEEN

Queen Eridu was deep in consultation with her Royal Ouija Board Operator when the Town Crier burst in to report the citywide traffic snarl. And this time he really was crying, because his brand-new pony cart had just been totaled and he didn't have any insurance. (Come to think of it, nobody did.)

The Queen called an emergency town meeting, and within the hour City Hall was filled to capacity with irate motorists, pedestrians, farmers, merchants, and the usual kooks and malcontents who often turn up at town meetings. A long line of complainants waited to vent their frustration as Queen Eridu, Salvo, and the Town Council listened with concern.

A tough-looking woman with a burlap scarf on her head was first. "As Chairperson of Sumerians for Slow Growth, I say we get rid of these things before they destroy our quality of life!"

A man on crutches was next. "My wife backed over my foot," he said.

"My neighbor keeps driving through my vegetable patch," said a woman brandishing a trowel.

"My son stopped doing his chores," said an exasperated mother. "He spends all his time in the garage, tinkering."

"Life used to be a lot simpler," said a wistful man.

"It's these crazy kids and their hopped-up carts," said a crusty grandmother.

Seated up on the stage next to the Queen, Salvo was getting impatient. He wanted to end the meeting and simply throw Hubert in jail. "That'd fix his wagon," he thought, sadly lacking the sense of humor required to recognize this as a perfectly acceptable, if accidental, joke. But Eridu seemed bent on hearing out every last complaint. He leaned over and whispered in her ear.

"Your Majesty, this entire problem could be resolved swiftly if you were to confiscate all wheeled vehicles and consign them to the army."

"But we don't have an army," she said.

"I've been meaning to talk with you about that."

Just then a roar went up from the assembled throng as Hubert was brought in by the Royal Guards.

When he reached the stage, the crowd erupted in a collective "Boo," which made Hubert feel pretty awful. He'd gotten used to people treating him as if he was somebody special. He looked to the Queen for sympathy, but even she seemed a bit frosty.

"So, Hubert. Your little invention appears to have

stirred up quite a bit of controversy. What do you have to say for yourself?"

He took a deep breath. "Well, Your Highness, it's like with anything new. You've gotta expect a few glitches."

A man spoke up from the floor. "A glitch? Is that what you call this?" he said, pointing to his neck brace.

Hubert turned to address the whole room. "You can't make an omelet without breaking a few eggs." (The omelet was another of Samarra's inventions. Before that, Gorp ate eggs with the shells still on.) "I know there've been problems here and there, some minor congestion, but I really think you're exaggerating—"

A ruddy-faced man jumped to his feet. "Oh, he does, does he? Let's show him!"

The mob surged forward. The neck-brace wearer and the ruddy-faced man grabbed Hubert's arms and dragged him outside.

The situation in the public square bore out the citizens' claims: a noisy, seething parking lot of fury and despair. Some drivers were blowing noisily into rams' horns; others punched each other silly. Two wagon drivers who had been trying to back into the same space all morning said terrible things about each other's mothers.

Hubert's eyes popped at the spectacle. "Wow," he said. "These things really *are* catching on!"

"No, duh," said Ruddyface. "The question is, what's the boy genius gonna do about it?"

Hubert searched the crowd for any sign of support or sympathy. Finding none, he hopped up onto a low wall, partly to get a better view and partly to get away from Ruddyface, who looked ready to take a poke at him.

As he beheld the chaos in the town square Hubert tried to tune out the noise so he could concentrate. What he saw was a lot of vehicles pointing in different directions. This made sense, as they all had different places to go. But what if he could get them pointed in the same direction? Even if it were only temporary, it would be a start. But how? He turned the problem around and around in his head, and around and around and around and around until—

"I have an idea!" Hopping down from the wall, he seized the nearest long, straight object: the crutch of the man whose wife had run over him. Luckily, she managed to steady her husband before he fell on his nose.

Hubert started sketching excitedly in the dirt with the crutch, explaining as he went. "See, if everyone goes around in the same direction, there won't be any crashes. For instance, you come in here, you go around, you come out here. Pretty cool, huh?"

Everyone stared blankly at the drawing. "Don't you see? It's a traffic circle," he explained.

The crowd parted, and the Queen stepped forward and took a long look at the design.

"I don't know. It feels somehow . . . incomplete."

"It's a circle, Queen. What could be more complete than that?"

The audience was starting to grumble again when a clear, strong voice rang out. "Hubert, you forgot to mention the most important part!" He looked up to see who had spoken. It was Uma.

"I did?" asked Hubert.

"Yes, of course," said Uma, coming through the crowd. "The statue."

"The statue . . . right. . . ." He had no idea what she was talking about.

"You know, Hubert," she continued confidently. "The statue of our beloved Queen Eridu, standing proud atop a grand pedestal, arms gracefully outstretched, ensuring safe travel for all!" She hadn't worked in sales all that time for nothing.

Hubert turned toward the Queen and was gratified to see a big smile blooming on her face. "Of course," she said. "A traffic circle. What a divine idea!"

Queen Eridu wasted no time in putting a team of Royal Sculptors to work creating yet another glorious monument to herself, and when it was finished, she had it placed atop a twenty-foot stone pillar at the center of the new traffic circle.

The concept worked just the way Hubert envi-

sioned it, and pretty soon there were traffic circles all over Sumeria. Hubert designed each one with specified entrances and exits and posted big black-on-yellow arrows to make sure everybody went the same way. He also suggested the radical idea that drivers keep to one side of the road on straightaways, greatly reducing head-on collisions.

Of course, even with the new rules and regulations, there was still the occasional fender bender. After several accidents involving small children driving large carts, Hubert came up with the idea of driver's licenses, which could only be held by those aged sixteen or older. When the Queen asked him how he had arrived at that specific number, he explained that sixteen was the numerological equivalent of the name "Eridu" when calculated in the Phrygian system and divided by two.

"Splendid," she said, never suspecting the real reason: Hubert had just celebrated his sixteenth birthday.

Gorp was, as usual, the lone holdout against all this progress. He refused to use the traffic circles and went out of his way to avoid them. His relationship with Hubert became increasingly distant. Their dinner conversation pretty much consisted of "Pass the pita" and "Are you going to finish that eel?"

They were father and son in name only. Or would have been, if they'd had last names.

SIXTEEN

Hubert was lying on a tropical island with his head in Uma's lap, shaded by a grove of palm trees. "You've got it all," she cooed. "Brains, vision, the admiration of your father, the love of a good woman, and the thanks of a grateful nation. Not to mention that magnificent, sculpted physique."

He stroked her long hair, and she popped a grape in his mouth. "Sorry," he said, "I didn't quite catch that. Would you mind repeating it?"

"Of course not. You've got it all, Hubert . . . Hubert . . . Hubert, wake up!"

At this point, the dream dissolved and Hubert awoke to find that he wasn't stroking Uma's hair, he was stroking Hodja's tail, and his head wasn't resting in her lap, but on the onager's chunky butt. He made a mental note to stop sharing his bed with the beast.

"Hubert, wake up," repeated Uma, but this time he wasn't dreaming it. She was actually there, standing right outside his window. He jumped out of bed. Luckily, he was already dressed in his street clothes, as pajamas wouldn't be invented for another twelve hundred years.

"I've been wanting to talk to you," he told her as he hoisted her in through the window. "That was pretty cool, the way you helped me out at the town meeting. That Queen can be a tough nut."

"It was nothing. Like I said, you've gotta give the customers what they want."

"How did you know what she wanted?"

"Are you kidding? Everybody knows the Queen has an edifice complex." She glanced around the cluttered room. "So this is where it all happens, huh?"

"The Queen gave me a workshop down at the palace, but I get more done here."

She toured the room, fascinated by all the fanciful gizmos and gewgaws. Wheels of various types and sizes were all over the place. On the dresser, Spike was enjoying his morning workout on the wire wheel in his cage.

"What are these?" she asked, bending over to examine a complicated-looking project that involved several buckets of water.

"Waterwheels. They let you capture energy from streams and rivers. Those are just models, the real ones'll be twenty times as big. They could run mills, factories, all sorts of stuff."

She liked how excited Hubert got when he talked about his work. It was like watching a kid open birthday presents. In one corner was a two-wheeled device that looked sort of like a modern-day golfer's pull cart. "How about this?" she asked.

"I designed that for my dad, to carry his clubs." He slipped three caveman-style clubs in the corresponding slots. "I sure hope he likes it."

"You really oughta get past the father issues, Hubert. You're practically an adult. You should assert yourself. Be your own man!"

"If I do, will you go out with me?"

"Can't, my dad won't let me. He doesn't even know I'm here. I told him I was going to a trade show."

"What's with that guy? He's making more money than ever, off *my* idea, and he treats me like I was some kind of disgusting reptile. No offense, Spike."

"Ah, he's just nursing a bruised ego. But I think I figured out a way to soften him up."

"Yeah?" Hubert said, brightening.

"Every man has his weakness. And believe me, I know my dad's."

A week later Hubert pulled up in front of Big Al's house in what can best be described as a machismobile. Following Uma's detailed instructions, he had custom-built for her father a two-wheeled racing chariot—the flashiest, gaudiest, most outrageous vehicle in all of Mesopotamia. It was Al's favorite color (candy-apple red) and featured pointy tail fins, high-gloss grillwork, oversized slicks, and pinstriped flames on either side.

Uma covered Big Al's eyes and led him out onto the porch. "Surprise!"

"Great leaping anaconda," he stammered, "you made this just for me?"

Hubert smiled. "Only a man like you could fully appreciate a vehicle like this." Circling the chariot in a daze, Al paused to run his hand over the rear spoiler and admire the twin mud flaps, each of which sported a figure of an alluring woman reclining on a beach. Hubert patted the seat next to him.

"Go ahead, Dad," said Uma.

Al approached the chariot reverently and stroked the seat. "Is that . . ."

"Yep," answered Hubert, anticipating the question. "Corinthian leather."

"Kid, you got style."

"Go ahead, take 'er for a spin."

Uma knew enough sales psychology to see that her father's resistance was at an all-time low. She could blow anything past him right now. "Hubert will help me close up the shop, okay?"

"Good man."

"And then he'd like to take me out on a date, all right?"

"Sure, whatever you say."

"Take your time. Don't hurry back."

"I won't." He pointed at the rear spoiler. "What does this do?"

"Nothing," Hubert said, handing him the reins. "But I thought you'd like it." He climbed down out of the driver's seat.

Moving as if in a dream, Big Al mounted the vehicle. He had never felt bigger in his life. He shook the reins, gave an exuberant "YEE-HA," and Hodja peeled out.

"Another satisfied customer," said Uma.

Now that Big Al was out of the way, Hubert and Uma closed up shop and headed to a nearby park for their first real, honest-to-goodness date. Hubert had never been on a date before, so he brought along some new inventions to test in case they ran out of things to talk about.

Until now, his wheeled contraptions had been mostly for business, but he had recently come up with a few that were just for fun. With a couple of minor modifications, he turned a wooden crate into a scooter and fashioned two pairs of workable roller skates out of old shoes.

He even managed to create a primitive bicycle, using a diamond-shaped frame the village blacksmith made for him. Hoisting Uma onto the handlebars, they rode together down to the river's edge, where another surprise was waiting: Hubert had patched a hole in an old fishing boat and attached paddle wheels to the sides. They hopped in, and Hubert pushed out onto the slow-moving river.

"How do you come up with all this stuff?" she asked once they were under way.

"I don't know. I guess I just think, 'wouldn't it be cool if,' and then I figure out a way to make it happen. And if it doesn't work, I just keep trying till it does."

"Pretty amazing," she said. He handed her a pinwheel he'd made out of ficus leaves. It made a soft, whirring sound as it turned in the breeze. "Don't take this the wrong way, Hubert, but it's kind of hard to believe you and your dad are related."

"I'm a lot more like my mom, really," he said. Then he told her all about Samarra and her various inventions: the high chair, the soupspoon, and, his personal favorite, gravy.

"You must really miss her," she said.

"Yeah."

"What happened to her?"

"Well, one of her inventions got a little out of control. See, she had this idea that shade should be portable, since you couldn't always count on finding a tree when you wanted to have a picnic. So she took some cloth and some wood and built a sort of collapsible awning on a stick. She called it the umbrella.

"But the first time we tried it out, it was a really windy day, and when she opened it, a big gust of wind picked her right up off the ground. She got caught in an updraft. Dad yelled for her to let go, but she hung on. I guess she'd worked so hard on it . . ."

He paused, gazing out across the water. "The last we saw her, she was disappearing over the horizon."

"That must have been tough on you," she said, taking his hand in hers.

"It was even tougher on my dad," he said. "And ever since that day he's been against new ideas of any kind. Especially the ones that come from me."

They pedaled in silence for a moment. Then Uma said, "I lost my mom, too."

"Really?"

"She was in a high-risk profession. Snake charmer."

"Wow," Hubert said.

"She played all the top clubs. She could hypnotize

any snake with just a few notes on her oboe. But one day she came up against the one thing that snake charmers fear most: a deaf cobra."

"Bummer," he said.

She put her head on his shoulder. This was a new sensation for Hubert. He suddenly felt strong and protective, and Uma's head felt a heck of a lot nicer than Hodja's butt.

SEVENTEEN

ig Al liked to drive fast, and the hot-rod cart
was built for speed. The sawed-off salesman
was really working Hodja into a lather—skid-
ding around tight corners, accelerating up steep hills,
zooming through deep valleys.

Hodja, who had disliked Big Al ever since the time
in the marketplace when the huckster referred to him
as a "pygmy pony," agreed only reluctantly to be part
of Hubert's plan, and only after Hubert had promised
to double Hodja's alfalfa ration and let him have the
good blanket for a month. But this loudmouth was
really getting on his nerves. In addition to driving like
a maniac, Al kept yelling things like "Gitalong" and
"Yippee-i-o-ki-ay!"

"What a dweeb," thought Hodja.

Cresting a hill, Big Al came up behind a convoy
of heavy, wide, slow-moving sledges and had to hit
the brakes hard to avoid rear-ending them. Al didn't
recognize any of the riders. Assyrians, he figured,
out for a Sunday drive on their sledge-osauruses.

"Hey, Gramps, let's move it," he hollered. "I got

things to do, places to go, people to take advantage of." But the sledges just kept moseying along. Al tailgated impatiently until they came to a straightaway, then whacked Hodja's haunches, and they whizzed past the whole convoy like a rocket. "Get with the times, slowpokes," he razzed before leaving them in his dusty wake.

Now miles from home, Big Al realized he was in the vicinity of the Border Bar & Grill, a funky roadhouse smack on the border between Sumeria and Assyria. The joint catered to a rough clientele: vagabonds, desperadoes, and assorted lowlifes on their way from nowhere-in-particular to don't-even-ask, who often stopped in for a drink, a show, and, if they were lucky, a bench-clearing brawl.

Al had been to the place once or twice in his

younger and wilder years, and he suddenly found himself in the mood for a cold brew.

"The perfect end to the perfect day," he said to Hodja as they pulled up in front. Seductive bump-and-grind music drifted out through the windows. Hot diggity, Al thought, Maud must be presenting one of her famous floor shows.

He swaggered into the bar like John Wayne, letting the swinging doors bang shut behind him, and took a seat at the granite bar next to a toothless old copper miner. The miner just wanted to enjoy the entertainment, "Velveeta and Her Vanishing Veils," but Al couldn't stop bragging about his new ride. "I tell ya, buddy, I've driven every heap that's ever been made. But when I parked my rump in that bucket seat . . . hey, I got 'er right out front, you wanna take a look?"

"Not just now, bub," answered the miner, his eyes never leaving the stage.

Al ordered a mug of home-brewed grog, and then another, blathering all the while about his road-racing victory over the Assyrians. "Man, you should've seen those troglodytes eat my dust." He elbowed the miner in the ribs. "Hey, here's a good one. How many Assyrians does it take to change a wall torch?" One. But he'll still be sitting in the dark."

"I don't get it," said the miner.

"'Cause Assyrians are so primitive, they haven't discovered fire yet, see? That's the joke."

A sudden silence came over the bar. The band

stopped playing, and the dancing girls scampered off-
stage. The miner muttered a nervous "gotta go" and
hustled out the door. "That's funny," thought Big Al,
"the joke wasn't *that* bad."

But what had silenced the bar was something else
altogether: A whole gang of ferocious-looking Assyrians had entered, and standing right behind Al
was the fearsome Ajax himself.

You could hear a pin drop as the warlord clamped
his viselike hand down on Big Al's shoulder and
slowly rotated him on his barstool. Al quickly recognized Ajax and his posse as the "slowpokes" he encountered earlier.

"Hey, guys," he began nervously. "How's it going? Nice day, isn't it? A little hot, admittedly. But it's
a dry heat."

Ajax just stared at the wheeler-dealer. Big Al
downed his drink and slid off the stool. "Well, it's
been absolutely grand chatting with you, gentlemen.
Must do it again sometime. Ta-ta."

But Al wasn't going anywhere. At Ajax's signal the
Assyrians formed a tight semicircle around him. The
warlord finally spoke, his voice low and menacing.
"Is that your rig parked out front?"

"Oh, that? Well, that's kind of an experiment. A
novelty, really. Pretty funny-looking, don't you think?"

"It didn't look so funny when you blew our doors
off back there."

"Oh, was that you?" He snapped his fingers. "I
thought you fellows looked familiar. Heh, heh, heh."

"Heh, heh, heh," repeated Ajax, uncoiling his whip. Big Al closed his eyes. He couldn't stand the sight of blood, especially his own.

"You wanna take this outside?" thundered Maud, the owner of the Border Bar & Grill, emerging from the back office on sturdy legs. She underlined the request by bringing her well-known, foot-long knife out of its sheath with a zing.

"No problem, Maud," said Ajax with a grin, grabbing Al by the scruff of the neck. "We'll take it outside."

Back at Big Al's house Hubert and Uma waited on the front-porch swing for his return. It had been dark for hours, and fireflies were winking in the night sky.

"It's kind of weird that they're not back yet," she said.

"Yeah, Hodja usually likes to hit the sack by ten."

"Maybe they're just having so much fun, they lost track of time."

"Yeah, probably."

It was well past Hodja's bedtime when he plodded up the driveway, wheezing with exhaustion. Big Al was riding on his back. The cart was nowhere to be seen.

"Dad! Where on earth have you been?" cried Uma.

"Where's the cart?" asked Hubert.

Noticing that her father's clothes were in tatters and he was covered with bumps, bruises, and scrapes, Uma jumped up from the swing and rushed to his side.

"What happened to you?" asked Uma.

"What happened to the cart?" asked Hubert.

Big Al glared at Hubert. "'What happened to the cart?' Is that all you can think of? Why, I nearly perished out there."

"You look awful," Uma said as she helped her father down from Hodja's back.

"Well, I shouldn't wonder, given the calamitous events I've been through tonight. It's a miracle I survived."

As Uma and Hubert helped him to the porch Big Al launched into his tale of woe.

"You see, Hodja and I were cruising along, observing posted speed limits of course, when suddenly we found ourselves pitching headlong down a perilous incline. Only my superb driving skills saved us from certain doom."

Hodja shot Al a dubious look, wishing more than ever that he could talk. Uma picked some bits of gravel out of her father's scraped elbow.

"We'd barely recovered from this episode," Al continued, "when we were set upon by a pack of rabid dogs, which threatened to tear us limb from limb. Following these attackers in quick succession were a gaggle of geese, a bevy of boa constrictors, and a swarm of bees."

Hodja was rolling his eyes so hard that he was in danger of dislocating them.

"I thought bees only flew during the day," Uma said, growing suspicious.

"Just the nice ones," Al replied, then took a deep breath and continued with renewed vigor. "It seemed we were home free when we encountered the deadliest hazard of all: quicksand. Cart and onager alike were sinking fast. Had I not exhibited the presence of mind to disconnect the harness, we might very well have lost precious little Hodja, too."

This was more than Hodja could bear. He made a hoof-down-the-throat gesture and walked away.

"Then the cart . . ." Hubert began.

"Alas, lost to posterity," Big Al said with a sniffle. "And to think of how hard you worked on it. . . ." He burst into sobs.

Hubert put an arm around him. "I can always make another one," he said. "The important thing is, everyone's okay." Al sneaked a look at his daughter to see how well his story had gone over. She folded her arms.

"A gaggle of geese, huh?"

"That's right. Vicious, bloodthirsty geese."

EIGHTEEN

Summer and fall flew by.

Hubert's life had improved considerably. He was the toast of the town; he liked his work; Big Al had lifted the ban on his friendship with Uma; and Jiff, Cliff, and Dirk were too busy learning stunts on their bikes and scooters to give him wedgies.

Sumerians were quickly adapting to life on wheels, almost to the point of taking them for granted. Crashes were down, and there were now body shops and personal injury lawyers for those "unlucky drivers." People obeyed most of the rules of the road most of the time, and for those who didn't, there was traffic school. It was widely agreed that things were better than they used to be.

Even the Assyrians seemed to be keeping to themselves. There hadn't been a raid for months.

Gorp didn't know what to make of all this peace and prosperity. Everything was going smoothly, just as his son had envisioned. The sky hadn't fallen. The world hadn't ended. He even caved in and had wheels attached to his Bronze Bomber, and within a day or

two he found himself wondering how he'd ever gotten along without them. It was hard to admit, even to himself, but he was developing a grudging respect for the kid.

And yet Gorp couldn't quite shake the feeling that all these "improvements" were too good to be true and that somehow, something terrible was going to happen.

NINETEEN

At last came the moment that every Sumerian had anxiously awaited: the completion of the Ziggurat. Queen Eridu declared a national day of celebration and invited all the residents of the Tigris-Euphrates Valley to the grand opening.

It really was a magnificent structure. The scaffolding and piles of building materials were gone, and the steep stone walls were painted a brilliant white. Surrounding the base were frescoes and colorful murals depicting great moments in the history of Ur, such as the coronation of Queen Eridu and the time Farmer Omar grew a stalk of rhubarb nearly six feet tall.

There was even a small mosaic portrait of Hubert near the entrance, which he found quite flattering except that the nose was too big.

Colorful banners danced in the breeze, and a huge purple one fluttered above the peak. A wide blue ribbon had been stretched across the main entrance.

The Royal Sumerian Marching Band, resplendent in dress uniforms, played festive tunes on drums, horns, and bone flutes as the entire population of the city gathered to witness the momentous event. On a raised platform near the main entrance, a row of dignitaries looked appropriately dignified. They applauded politely when Salvo approached the podium.

"Citizens of Ur!" he began. "I humbly present Her Majesty, the most exalted Queen Eridu, ruler and protector of the good people of Sumeria."

In the spirit of the day, the Queen had chosen to make her grand entrance in the new Royal Carriage that Hubert designed. It was even more extravagant than the cart he built for Big Al: sunroof, tuck-and-roll upholstery, six wheels with copper spokes. At eighteen feet long, it was nearly impossible to parallel park.

The crowd whooped with delight when the carriage rolled to a stop in front of the viewing platform and Queen Eridu emerged dressed in the finest silk and satins. She mounted the marble steps to a lively fanfare. Salvo stood aside with a sweeping bow, and the crowd fell silent, eager to hear their beloved Queen speak.

"When Prime Minister Salvo gave me my first Ouija Board and instructed me in its use, I was much surprised to learn that it was my destiny to build a great Ziggurat for the people of Ur. I was also much dismayed, as I did not know what a Ziggurat was. But when Salvo explained to me the building's many possible uses—meeting place, concert hall, day-care facility, playground, post office, health spa—I gladly accepted the challenge. And now it is my great pleasure to present it to its rightful owners, the fine and brave and clever and deserving people of Sumeria!"

The crowd cheered wildly. They'd worked very hard on the Ziggurat and were looking forward to enjoying its many attractions.

"But first, I must give credit to a very special person," she went on, "thanks to whose ingenuity this gargantuan project was completed under budget and well ahead of schedule. And in honor of his contribution, I've invited him to cut the ribbon declaring the Ziggurat open to one and all. Ladies and gentlemen, I give you—Hubert!"

Hubert took the stage to a rousing ovation. Salvo handed him a three-foot-long pair of ceremonial scissors, and he carried them to the podium.

"Thanks, Queen," he began. "This is really everybody's accomplishment, but I especially want to thank a few people. My mom, who gave me the gift of creativity, . . . my best friend, Uma, who helped steer me in the right direction, . . . but most of all, I want to thank my dad, who never stood in my way, who was always there for me, and who always believed in me."

The part about his dad wasn't entirely true, of course. Gorp had fought Hubert nearly every inch of the way, was rarely there for him, and often doubted him. But Hubert so badly wanted it to be true that as he said the words he almost convinced himself.

"So, I'd like to ask him to come up here and cut this ribbon with me. What do you say, Dad?"

He looked down into the audience to where his father stood. Gorp was a bundle of mixed emotions. But the crowd's applause and shouts of encouragement acted like a big, warm tidal wave that lifted him right up onto the platform, and the next thing he knew he was standing next to his son, with a huge grin on his face.

Hubert smiled right back at him. "Here, Dad," he said, handing him the giant scissors. "Why don't you do the honors?"

This small gesture melted Gorp's heart. With deep fatherly pride, something he hadn't felt for Hubert in an achingly long time, he put out his hands, and . . .

Something rumbled.

It was a low, menacing rumble, like a distant thunderstorm, or an earthquake, or the stomach of a lion who hadn't eaten for a long, long time. Everyone felt it.

"Excuse me, what was that?" asked the Queen.

The crowd turned to see where it was coming from, but it seemed to be coming right out of the earth itself. And it was getting louder.

"Look! Over there!" yelled a tall man. Everyone turned to see what he was pointing at.

A cloud had formed off to the north. It wasn't like any cloud anybody had ever seen before. It was on the ground, not in the sky, and it was brown, not white. And it was approaching very fast.

"We're under attack!" hollered Salvo.

Now the cloud split into several distinct clouds, all of them coming straight toward Ur. "Man the barricades," Salvo ordered, but there wasn't time. The first of the Assyrian war chariots had already entered the city.

"Holy mackerel, they've got the wheel," somebody cried.

TWENTY

There were twelve war chariots in all. Each was drawn by four fast, powerful horses, and each held six soldiers in full battle gear, brandishing swords, clubs, spears, maces—an entire arsenal of primitive weaponry. Driving the lead chariot was Ajax himself, clutching the reins of his four steeds with one hand and madly cracking his whip with the other.

The chariots streamed into the square at top speed and circled the terrified crowd as the soldiers whooped and jeered. A soldier wielding a battle-ax cut the legs out from under the viewing stand, sending the Queen, Salvo, Hubert, Gorp, and the dignitaries tumbling to the ground. The awning floated down over them, plunging them all into darkness. "The indignity of it all!" wailed Queen Eridu.

From one end of town to the other, the Assyrians were doing what they did best—wreaking havoc—only they did it much more effectively on rolling stock. One chariot defiled the Garden of Peace and Freedom, crushing the Queen's beloved lilacs beneath its massive wheels. Another clattered down the middle of Main Street, brazenly violating the keep-to-the-right rule. Terrified Sumerians leaped out of the way as it barreled along, scattering fruit stands and café tables.

Another chariot driver cackled with glee as he terrorized the Royal Sumerian Marching Band, pursuing them up and down the narrow streets like a cat going after a family of mice. One of his soldiers grabbed a drum and jammed it over the drummer's head. Another swiped a lute and wrapped it around the lute player's neck.

Chaos reigned supreme.

In the town square, the former occupants of the viewing stand fought their way out from under the tarp only to find themselves face-to-face with Ajax, who stood tall in the lead chariot, his massive jaw set like the cornerstone of the Ziggurat itself. The rest of the Assyrians assembled behind him in battle formation.

"We shall return," Ajax thundered, raising his whip. "When we do, you will surrender your land, your crops, and your water. And if you don't, may the gods have mercy on you. Because *we* won't!"

At his signal the raiding party moved out with a terrible clatter of hooves, but not before Ajax led the chariots in a victory lap around the traffic circle. Lashing out with his whip, he snared the statue of the Queen by its delicate neck and toppled it, smashing it to pieces.

With a throaty victory cry the Assyrians departed,

passing quite close to Uma, who had taken refuge behind a stone wall. For the first time she got a close look at the chariots. Every one was candy-apple red with tail fins, a spoiler, and a pair of mud flaps decorated with a reclining beach bunny.

"Dad?" she called out in an accusing tone. He popped his head out of the barrel he'd been hiding in.

"Yes, dear?"

She gave him a long, cold stare. "Quicksand, huh?"

He climbed out of the barrel, dusting himself off. "You wouldn't rat on your own father, would you?" he pleaded. "I'm the only family you've got."

"Don't remind me," she said, turning her back to him.

Queen Eridu and the stunned dignitaries silently surveyed the wreckage. No one knew what to say.

Hubert rushed to her side, pausing briefly to pick up a heavy, roundish object: the head of the destroyed statue. He tucked it under his arm like a football and addressed the crowd in the manner of a coach whose team is down 49–0 at halftime.

"Okay," he said, "this is a setback. But I think if we all pull together, we can clean up this mess and . . ." He trailed off, becoming aware of the hostile glares of everyone present. It was a look he knew well by now.

When he handed the Queen her own head, she burst into tears. "Why wasn't I warned of this?" she sobbed. "My horoscope said nothing! Where is my Royal Soothsayer?" She staggered off in search of him.

Now Hubert heard a different kind of rumble. It was the sound of his fellow citizens—the same citizens who had been his biggest fans a few minutes earlier—turning into his harshest critics. Searching for a trace of sympathy, he found nothing but hatred and accusation.

"Dad?" he said, spotting his father among the crowd.

Gorp just shook his head and said, "You happy now?" then walked away.

"Wait a minute," Hubert pleaded to the towns-people. "There's no need to panic! Maybe we can negotiate with the Assyrians. Ajax seems like a reasonable guy—a little rough around the edges, admittedly, but . . ." He trailed off, realizing that nobody wanted to hear what he had to say.

The Queen was dazed and confused. The dignitaries were paralyzed by hopelessness and despair. The townspeople were terrified. Salvo had been waiting his whole life for this moment: a power vacuum. He stepped into it.

"This is no time for weakness," he said in a voice that carried with it the unmistakable conviction of a man with a mission. "I am in charge here."

All eyes were on the Prime Minister as he elbowed Hubert aside, drew his long sword, and held it above his head. "I hereby declare martial law . . . and I hereby annex this Ziggurat as my military headquarters. FOLLOW ME!"

Salvo spoke the last two words with such authority that everyone within earshot—men, women, and children—simply fell in behind him. Moving with purpose and vigor, the absurd days of fetching Hubert's lunch behind him at last, he strode up the steps and sliced the blue ribbon in two.

He continued upward, now at the head of a growing parade of frightened, obedient Sumerians. Hubert watched helplessly as they passed him, lemminglike, and filed into the dark opening of the Ziggurat.

TWENTY-ONE

In a few short weeks Salvo had transformed the Ziggurat from a public meeting place into a bustling military headquarters and weapons factory—which was, of course, what he wanted all along. Everyone was working around the clock to prepare for the coming war against Assyria. Women forged swords and stoked fires, men assembled war chariots, children sharpened blades on grinding wheels.

The Prime Minister was truly in his element at last. Striding through his factory, he breathed in the fragrances of sweat, smoke, and fear as if they were wildflowers.

"Keep up the pace, kiddies, a true patriot never tarries," he chirped to a table of children fitting handles into battle-ax blades. Snatching a crust of bread away from a scrawny orphan, he added, "None of that, now. There'll be time enough for snacks once we've defeated the Hun."

Hubert was down in the bowels of the Ziggurat designing a siege engine. A siege engine is a weapon that flings boulders long distances in order to squash enemies or destroy their forts. It's big, brutish, and highly effective. This kind of technology wasn't really to Hubert's taste, but what choice did he have? Everybody worked for Salvo now.

"Way to go, jerk," sneered Jiff as he and his fellow Punks shuffled past, lugging a twenty-foot-long battering ram.

"Got any other bright ideas?" said Cliff.

"Couldn't just stick with the water jugs, could you?"

"Believe me, I wish I had."

As the trio vanished down a dark tunnel Dirk's voice echoed off the walls: "Egghead."

It wasn't just the Punks who blamed Hubert; everyone did. If Mister Know-It-All hadn't invented the wheel, they reasoned, then the Assyrians couldn't have stolen it, which meant they couldn't have used it to attack the Sumerians, which meant the Sumerians wouldn't have had to defend themselves, which meant everything would have been beer and skittles instead of pain and misery. This argument conveniently ignored Big Al's loss of his chariot, the Assyrians' need for food and water, Ajax's bad temper, and Salvo's lust for power, but just dumping all the blame on Hubert had the advantage of being nice and simple.

He was pondering his predicament when Salvo glided up behind him.

"How's my siege engine coming?" he asked.

"Okay, I guess," said Hubert, showing him the

drawing. "But with these minor modifications, it'd make a great fruit harvester—"

Salvo snatched the sketch away and tore it up. "Let's try to keep our eye on the ball, shall we?" he barked. "I've got a war to win here."

"Hey, this place was supposed to be a community center."

Salvo patted him on the head. "Right you are, Hubert. And civil defense is a community project."

"There was going to be day care, and a gym—"

"Our children are being closely monitored, and their parents are getting the workout of a lifetime!"

There was no arguing with this guy. Hubert started in on a new design, but Salvo handed him an oilcan.

"Listen, I want you to go down to the basement and grease that treadwheel."

"Which one?"

"The squeaky one. Duh."

Hubert's workstation was deep in the Ziggurat, but there was one more level below his. This was the hottest, stuffiest, darkest, smelliest, smokiest room in the whole place: the power plant.

All the heavy machinery in the Ziggurat was powered by drive belts that came up through slots in the floor. At the other ends of the belts were treadwheels—giant versions of the one Hubert had installed in Spike's cage. Row upon row of these devices turned day and night, and inside each one toiled a single huffing, puffing laborer.

Hubert descended the stone steps to the power plant, where his ears quickly led him to the offending wheel. His heart sank when he saw that its operator was none other than his own father.

While oiling the axle, Hubert tried to strike up a light conversation. "Hey, Dad, how's it going?" No answer. "Hot enough for you?" Nothing. "You can really work up a nice sweat down here, huh?" Gorp wouldn't even make eye contact; he just kept walking.

"Listen," Hubert continued, "I'm really sorry about the way things turned out."

The wheel stopped revolving. "So, you're sorry,"

Gorp said angrily. "Are you as 'sorry' as you were the day you flooded the house? Are you as 'sorry' as the time you made me canvas underwear for Father's Day? Or maybe you're as 'sorry' as you were when you tried out your new manure spreader—in the living room! Or the time you made me a bed warmer and burned all the hair off my back?"

"But, Dad—"

"Yeah, you're sorry, all right," he said, returning to his labors. "You're a sorry excuse for a son."

Crushed, Hubert watched him for a moment before leaving. There was nothing more to say.

TWENTY-TWO

The north road out of Ur was once a busy artery for farmers, merchants, and commuters, but on the day Hubert decided to leave home forever, he had it all to himself. Everybody in Sumeria was busy making weapons, fortifying the city, or drilling with the newly formed Sumerian Army.

"I'm a man without a country, guys," he said to Hodja, on whose back he was riding, and Spike, who straddled the tuft on Hodja's head. Hubert had left the cart and his toolbox back at the house; all they ever did was cause trouble.

"Dad was right. I should've gone into the hauling business. I wouldn't have been much, but I would've been somebody. Instead of a bum. Which is what I am."

The sun was setting when the Border Bar & Grill came into view up ahead, dark and sinister in the fading light. Hubert pulled Hodja up short.

"Wow. The Border Bar and Grill. I've heard stories about this place, Hodja. Wild women. Desperate men.

Violence, drunkenness, and debauchery." His face became a grim mask of resolve. "That's for me."

Attempting a manly swagger, Hubert pushed through the swinging doors and entered the crowded room. There they were, all right: a bunch of rowdy tough guys, drinking, cussing, carousing, and spitting on the floor. He dragged a stool up to the granite bar. Maud lumbered over and plunked a coaster in front of him.

"What'll it be, bub?"

"Gimme a grog, honey," he said with all the gruffiness he could muster. "And keep 'em coming."

"I'm gonna need to see some ID."

He handed her his new driver's license, hoping she wouldn't notice that he'd chiseled a few extra lines in to bump up his age.

She noticed.

"Nice try, kid. Now get lost," Maud growled, jerking her thumb toward the door. Hubert slipped off the stool and slunk away, but his exit was blocked by the arrival of a gang of Assyrians. Hubert drew a sharp breath when he recognized their dreaded leader, Ajax.

As the Assyrians filed in, Hubert ducked behind a pillar to eavesdrop. Colonel Karp was explaining something to two of the soldiers, a tall, skinny one and a short, stocky one.

"See, Stretch, once they know we've got it, they

have to comply," Karp said. "'Cause if they don't, they know we'll use it. That's what you call 'deterrence.'"

Stretch looked confused. "So if they comply, does that mean we don't get to use it?"

"Right," said Karp.

Plug, the stocky one, looked disappointed. "After we went to all that trouble to make it?"

Karp rubbed his chin. "That *would* be kind of anticlimactic, wouldn't it?"

Hubert knew he should get out of there fast, but he had to know what the "it" was that these guys were talking about. He doubled back and found a hiding place near the bar.

Ajax, noticing that another customer occupied his favorite stool, casually dumped him on the ground and claimed it for himself. Karp took the seat next to him, and the rest of the crew settled in.

"Do you really think it'll work?" asked Karp.

"Of course it'll work. Those Sumerian nitwits will never know what hit 'em."

"What the heck is 'it,'" wondered Hubert, edging closer, but at that moment Maud picked him up by the scruff of the neck.

"Does your dad know where you are, sonny?"

"No. And he doesn't care."

"You're breakin' my heart," she said, before tossing him out the door like a stray cat.

Hubert rolled to a stop in the dusty road. Driven by curiosity, he sprang to his feet and started searching for another way into the building. He soon found one: a window above the stage door. Through it he could clearly see Ajax and his men at the bar, but couldn't quite make out what they were saying.

Just then, two chorus girls arrived from the parking lot. Chorus girls, then as now, were tall, beautiful dancers with great expertise at entertaining the type of guy that hung out at joints like the Border Bar & Grill. One of them spotted Hubert peering through the window.

"Hey, junior. If you're here for the show, you're a little early."

"Yeah, about five years early," giggled the other one. The girls went in through the stage door, closing it in his face. But they'd given him an idea.

A s you might expect of a fellow who lived alone in a cave, Ajax was just wild about chorus girls. He muscled his way into a front-row seat as Maud mounted the stage to whistles and catcalls.

"Silence," she demanded, one hand on the butt of her well-respected knife. "Silence, you animals! Well, we all know why you're here, and it ain't the decor nor the cuisine. So without further ado, the Border Bar and Grill is proud to present—the Seven Sirens of the Nile!"

The house band kicked in, and out came the Sirens, alluringly dressed in harem pants, sheer scarves, and tall, glittery headdresses. Colored veils obscured everything but their heavily made-up eyes.

Karp elbowed Ajax in the ribs. "Hey, Chief. If they're called the Seven Sirens of the Nile, how come there are eight of 'em? Pretty dumb, huh?"

Karp happened to be right, even though math was never his strong suit. In fact, he couldn't count higher than ten without taking off his shoes. But at the moment Ajax couldn't have cared less, because his entire attention was focused on the chorus girl on the end— the short, coquettish one who kept batting her eyes at him from behind her silky veil; the one who wasn't much of a dancer, if you looked closely; the one who was definitely hitting on him.

"I think she likes you," Colonel Karp giggled.

Gyrating to the edge of the stage, the petite dancer invited Ajax to join her. The tribal chief proved to be surprisingly light on his feet, and the routine ended to riotous applause. "I'm gonna buy that girl a drink," he decided.

Ajax sent a note backstage after the show, and before you could say Bob Fosse, he and the chorus girl were at the bar, deep in conversation.

"I've never met a real live warlord before," said Hubert in a feminine tone (for, as the astute reader has no doubt guessed by now, it was in reality our young hero underneath all that mascara and chiffon). "It must be fascinating work you do."

Hubert's makeup itched, his false eyelashes tickled, and his high heels were killing him, but he was determined to extract some information, no matter what the cost.

"Oh, just the usual," Ajax said. "You know, plundering, sacking. A little pillaging when I can find the time. What did you say your name was again?"

"Huber . . . ah . . . tina. Hubertina," said Hubert. He stole a glance up at the high window, where Hodja and Spike anxiously watched his every move.

"Those greedy Sumerians must really grate on your nerves."

"They won't for long, dollface," he said, gnawing on a pickled pig's foot. "I've got big plans for them."

"Do tell."

Ajax edged his stool a little closer to the showgirl. "I'd rather talk about *you,* sweetie," he purred. "Let's see what's under that pretty little veil." Before Hubert could stop him, Ajax whipped it away . . .

"Eek!" said Hubert.

. . . revealing another veil. Ajax donned a sly smile. "Playing hard-to-get, eh? I like a girl with spunk."

Hubert tried to keep Ajax on message. "Tell me more about your 'big plans.' I bet they're very clever."

"Well, actually, I did come up with them myself. Are you really interested in this kind of thing?"

"Terribly," Hubert cooed.

Ajax brought a piece of coal from his pocket and started drawing on the bar. "See, here are the mountains, where I live, and here's the valley—"

"Where those nasty Sumerians live."

"That's right, toots. Now what we've done is, we've created a little surprise for the nasty Sumerians, which will soon be arriving by special delivery." He looked up from the drawing. "Come on, honey, give me a peek. I can't stand it anymore."

He pulled away the second veil, revealing a third. It was a good thing Hubert found that box full of veils in the dressing room.

"Why, you little vixen." He reached for the third and final veil, but Hubert blocked the move.

"Not until you tell me what the surprise is. I just love surprises."

"Oh, all right," Ajax pouted. "I shouldn't be telling you this. But suffice it to say, tomorrow morning, this rock is gonna roll."

Hubert took a good look at the sketch. Ajax wasn't much of a draftsman, but the structure and purpose of the "surprise"—the "it" that the Assyrians had talked about earlier—was horrifyingly clear: The entire mountaintop had been carved into a gigantic wheel, and the city of Ur was right in its path.

Hubert was so shocked, he forgot himself and spoke in his normal guy voice.

"I've gotta get going."

Ajax's expression went from surprise to disappointment to rage in three seconds flat. He yanked away the final veil, exposing Hubert's face. Rage turned to fury as Ajax realized he'd been duped. "A spy!" he roared.

The barroom brawl that ensued would go down as the second worst in the Border's history, right behind the time Maud ran out of grog on a 120-degree afternoon. Kicking off the high heels, Hubert led the warlord and his gang on a merry chase, darting between chairs, under tables, and around pillars. Hindered by the billowing harem pants but spurred on by the will to live, he managed to stay a step ahead of his pursuers, racing across the stage, down dark hallways, and through crowded storerooms.

At one point, trapped between Plug and Stretch, he had no choice but to leap up onto the bar. He raced along it as Ajax bore down on him, swinging a heavy club. Each blow missed Hubert by inches, smashing the stone bar into foot-wide chunks.

Leaping down from the far end of the bar, he found himself cornered. Ajax advanced menacingly, five of his henchmen close behind. "This is for making me dance with you," he said, raising the club high.

For Spike, who had been watching the melee through the window above the stage door, the time to act was at hand. He jumped down from his perch and streaked across the dirt floor, and an instant before Ajax could deliver a crushing blow with the club, scrambled up inside one of the warlord's pant legs.

Ajax froze. Something weird was going on in his pants, and whatever it was, it wasn't good. Panicking, he swung the club and smashed himself between the legs five times in rapid succession. Spike ran out the other cuff, unharmed, and climbed into Hubert's pocket.

Only now did Ajax realize what he'd done to himself. "Ooouuuhhh," he said, and collapsed like a leaky balloon.

The rest of the Assyrians, now leaderless, looked in dismay toward the front doors, through which Hodja came galloping at warp speed, eyes wide, nostrils flaring. He lowered his head and plowed into the group like a linebacker, scattering Karp, Stretch, Plug, and the rest all over the room.

Hodja executed a neat 180 and returned for his partner. Spotting a particular chunk of the demolished bar at his feet, Hubert snatched it up and jumped onto Hodja's back, and the trio hastily put some distance between themselves and the Border Bar & Grill.

Half a mile down the road, they pulled over to catch their breath. Even Spike, who was riding in Hubert's pocket, was panting—mostly from fear. "Good work, team," Hubert said as he dismounted.

Now he took a closer look at the section of the granite bar that he'd picked up: the one bearing Ajax's drawing of the doomsday machine.

"What do you think, Hodja? Could anybody really make a wheel that big?" He scanned the mountains to the north for evidence of Ajax's evil plan, but all he saw was the familiar jagged skyline. Maybe it was just a story, he thought, a tall tale told by a warlord hoping to impress a beautiful showgirl. Maybe there was nothing to worry about. . . .

Then he saw it. Once you knew what you were looking for, it was obvious. Painfully so. Backlit by the rising moon, the outline of a wheel was visible—the most enormous wheel imaginable. And it was aimed directly at the heart of the city of Ur.

Hubert did a few calculations in his head and concluded that if Ajax released the weapon, it would be big enough, heavy enough, and moving fast enough to flatten most of the city and most of the people in it.

He had to warn them.

TWENTY-THREE

It was after midnight when Hubert, Hodja, and Spike arrived on the outskirts of Ur. The valiant onager had kept up a pace that would go unequaled until Paul Revere's famous ride, nearly fifty centuries later.

In the good old days Hubert would have taken a problem like this to his father, but their present relationship rendered this course of action pointless. He'd have to go straight to the powers that be. True, his credibility was shot, but at least the picture Ajax had drawn provided some proof of the dastardly plot.

"We're almost there, boy," Hubert urged his trusty steed. But as they rounded a corner, Hubert found his way blocked by three armed sentries.

"Halt! Who goes there?" said the first one. Hubert sagged when he recognized the trio as Jiff, Cliff, and Dirk, decked out in their new military uniforms.

"Aw, geez. Not you guys," Hubert said. Hodja bared his teeth at Dirk. He'd been dying to get another crack at this punk ever since the tail-pulling episode.

"Be you friend or foe?" said Cliff, brandishing a long staff. "Show yourself." Cliff's voice was changing, and it cracked, undermining the macho effect he was going for.

"Come off it, Cliff. It's me, Hubert. You've known me since we were little."

Jiff gave him the once-over. "Whaddaya know, it *is* Hubert."

Cliff strode up to him. "How come you're dressed like that? Did you switch teams?" It was a fair question—Hubert had been too busy riding to the rescue to change out of the gauzy pants and silk blouse.

"I'll explain later," he answered, hopping down from the onager and doffing the showgirl attire.

"Hey, Hubes," Dirk taunted, "I never noticed what beautiful eyes you have."

"I don't have time for this, you guys. I have to see Salvo—"

"What for?" asked Cliff. "You wanna date him?" He high-fived his two buddies. What a wit.

"I have to show him something," Hubert said, trying to stay calm. "We're about to be attacked."

"Lemme see what you got there," Cliff demanded. He snatched the flat stone from Hubert. "What is this? This doesn't make any sense."

"You're holding it upside down, nimrod." Hubert moved to take it back, but Cliff tossed the stone over his head to Dirk, kicking off a game of keep-away that lasted until Cliff's second throw went astray and the drawing shattered on the cobblestones.

"Nice work, guys. You've done a great service to your country." He jumped onto Hodja and rode off toward the city center.

"Hey, Hubert! I never noticed what a cute butt you have," Jiff called after him.

Hubert galloped straight to the Ziggurat, where he found no more success than he had with the Punks. The sentinels posted out front wouldn't even talk to him—they just pointed to the mosaic of Hubert's face, now circled in red with a bold diagonal line across it.

There was one last chance: Queen Eridu herself. Breathlessly arriving at the Royal Palace, Hubert tried to talk his way past her spear-carrying palace guards. "I'm telling you, I need to see the Queen!"

"The Queen is sequestered in a spiritual retreat concerning the fate of the Sumerian people," said the chief guard.

"*I'm* the one who can tell her the fate of the Sumerian people," Hubert insisted.

"Are you a clairvoyant?"

"No."

"Astrologer?"

"No."

"Tarot card reader?"

"No!"

"Well, those *are* the big three."

Hubert was getting nowhere. He made a desperate dash between the guards, but they crossed their spears, barring his entrance. He felt like his head was about to explode. "This is a matter of life and death! I have information of the utmost urgency! I'm sure that if you tell the Queen I'm here, she'll want to know what I have to say!"

No response. Hubert tried a final gambit. "As Royal Technologist, I order you to let me pass!"

The chief guard reached out and touched Hubert's cheek. Some rouge came off on his finger.

"Hey, kid," he said. "Are you wearing makeup?"

There is no alternative but to tackle this problem head-on, Hubert concluded as he mounted his steed. They would have to venture into territory where not even the bravest Sumerian had ever set foot: the Zagros Mountains.

TWENTY-FOUR

The steep, jagged mountains looked fairly spooky even from miles away, but halfway up the tallest peak in the dead of night, with only Hodja and Spike to keep him company, Hubert found them nothing short of terrifying.

He tried to fortify himself with some tough-guy talk. "Hodja, we've been through a lot together. But now we face our ultimate challenge. It's just you and me against an entire army of desperate, violent men."

This was enough for Hodja, who did an abrupt about-face and started back down the path; but with an artful combination of threats and promises, Hubert managed to get him back on course.

They climbed and climbed and climbed, a tiny speck against the steep cliffs, finally arriving at a wide, flat spot just below the peak. In the moonlight Hubert saw that the ground was littered with tools and rubble, the apparent aftermath of a massive construction project. But where was the giant wheel? Had they somehow climbed the wrong mountain?

Hearing noises from up ahead, Hubert dismounted and crept toward their source. He reached a high granite wall and peeked around it. Below him was a sprawling military encampment, eerily lit by flickering torches and smoky campfires. Hundreds of Assyrian soldiers were strapping on armor and weapons in preparation for a cataclysmic battle.

Hodja and Spike arrived at his side. "They're mobilizing," Hubert said. "Looks like we're just in time to . . . do something. . . ."

At the sudden sound of footsteps approaching from the rear, Hubert froze. He couldn't go forward and he couldn't go back. Spotting a crevice near the wall's base, he shoved Spike in his shirt pocket, dived into the crack, and hauled Hodja in after him.

An instant later two Assyrian soldiers arrived. "Just the little ones," said one. "They burn better."

Peering out, Hubert recognized the soldiers as Stretch and Plug, whom he'd encountered at the Border Bar & Grill. They appeared to be gathering firewood.

"Hey, Plug," Stretch said. "What do you call a Sumerian who stays in his apartment tomorrow? A flat dweller. Get it? Flat . . . dweller."

The soldiers continued to gather wood and swap highly insulting Sumerian jokes. Once they were gone, Hubert emerged from the crevice.

"Okay, Hodja, the first thing we have to do is figure out where that wheel is. It's not like they could be hiding it someplace." They tiptoed along the granite wall in the dark.

Hodja stopped in his tracks, wide-eyed with fear. "What is it, boy?" asked Hubert. Following the onager's gaze, he looked straight up . . . and his stomach plunged when he realized that the wall they'd been walking alongside was, in fact, one side of the wheel itself—a massive disk of solid rock, balanced on its edge, so tall that its top seemed to scrape the night sky.

"Uh-oh," said Hubert.

Spike, meanwhile, was on a mission of his own. Soon after the three musketeers reached the mountaintop, the lizard had smelled a familiar, intoxicating aroma drifting through the air. Now he slipped out of Hubert's pocket unnoticed and made straight for the source of the smell. Scrambling over boulders and stumps, he came upon Plug and Stretch's unattended campfire. A cauldron bubbled above it. Yum. He unhinged his jaw and dived right in.

A moment later the two soldiers returned, their arms loaded with firewood. "Dung-beetle soup," Plug groused. "Night after night it's the same old thing. Don't you know how to cook anything else?"

"Hey, it's not my fault scorpions are out of season. Tell you what, once we take the valley, I'll make you a fig frappé. In the meantime, shut up and eat."

Helping himself to a big ladleful of stew, Plug was astonished to find a pair of bulging eyes staring him in the face. Spike got one look at Plug, launched himself from the ladle, and took off like a bullet.

"What the heck was that?" asked Stretch.

"Who cares? It's got meat on it!" With that, the two soldiers followed in hot pursuit.

Back at the base of the humongous wheel, Hubert couldn't help but admire the Assyrians' ingenuity. Sure, they'd created a weapon of mass destruction, but what workmanship! The device was thousands of times larger than anything he'd attempted, yet almost perfectly round and expertly balanced. Two large chocks at its base—basically six-foot-long doorstops—were all that kept it from rolling down from its perch. By pulling out the chocks with the aid of a system of ropes and pulleys, one or two people could wreak havoc in the valley below.

"Very impressive," Hubert said to himself as he fingered the block and tackle. "Compounding the rope segments multiplies the force exerted on the load. That generates a huge mechanical advantage."

Hubert was so intrigued by the clever design, he didn't notice that Stretch and Plug were headed his way, in pursuit of what they hoped would be a part of tonight's balanced meal.

"Hey," yelled Stretch, catching sight of the intruders. "What are you doing here?"

Startled, Hubert straightened up quick. Spike zoomed up his leg and sought refuge in his shirt pocket.

Hubert weighed his options. Stretch and Plug were closing in fast. To his left was the vertical face of the wheel; to his right, a sheer drop of a hundred feet. The only way out was straight through the enemy camp, which meant almost certain capture. Finding none of these options very appetizing, Hubert stood rooted to the spot.

Hodja made a command decision. Ducking his head between Hubert's legs, he scooped him up onto his back, executed a quick U-turn, and took off at top speed into the camp.

Stretch and Plug's cries soon alerted the rest of the soldiers, making Hodja's job even harder. But an onager can really move when he has to, and by zigzagging like a quarter horse, he managed to slalom between the surprised Assyrians, eluding their hands and weapons.

All Hubert could do was hang on for dear life.

They were only a dozen yards short of a clean escape when a telltale *crack* split the night air. With deadly accuracy Ajax wrapped his whip around Hubert's waist, neatly plucked him from Hodja's back, and reeled him in like a sockeye salmon. Hodja looked back at his fallen comrade, but Hubert shooed him away. "Go, Hodja! Get help!"

Hodja kicked in the afterburners, lowered his head, smashed between a final pair of burly Assyrian soldiers, and vanished.

TWENTY-FIVE

Tied to a stake in the middle of the camp, Hubert found himself once again face-to-face with the Assyrian warlord. And this time without a veil.

"Well," Ajax said with a snort. "If it isn't the lovely and talented Hubertina. What brings you all the way up here?"

Hubert stared straight into the giant's beady eyes. "You forgot to tip me."

Ajax pulled him closer. "Yeah? Well, here's a tip for you: You spy, you die."

The other soldiers gathered around the prisoner, each drawing a club, knife, or sword. They knew well Ajax's approach to justice: summary execution, followed by sentencing, a fair trial, and, time permitting, arrest.

"Bye-bye," said Ajax, raising his hand to give the signal.

"Hey," Hubert said. "The least you could do is apologize."

Ajax could hardly believe the youth's impudence. "For what? I'm a warlord. I'm just doing my job."

"You're totally clueless," Hubert said. "You're as bad as Salvo."

"I beg your pardon?"

Hubert looked up at the disk of doom, which loomed above them like a monstrous bird of prey. "I had a great idea," Hubert went on. "It would have made everybody's life easier and better. But then people like you and him came along and ruined it for everybody. People like you stink."

The soldiers gasped. They'd never heard anyone mouth off to Ajax like that. Colonel Karp, finally

showing some aptitude for math, put two and two together.

"Hey," said Colonel Karp. "I bet this is that kid who invented the wheel."

"Sure, rub it in," Hubert said.

The rest of the troops were still standing with weapons poised, awaiting Ajax's command; but their leader, amazingly, started laughing.

"What a delicious irony! You set out to help your fellow countrymen, yet your creation is about to result in their destruction!"

He laughed until his sides hurt. Finally one of the soldiers, straining under the weight of a ten-pound mace, spoke up.

"Pardon me for interrupting, sir, but do you want us to execute this kid or what?"

All at once Ajax grew serious. "Lock him up in the stockade."

"Alive, sir?" asked the puzzled soldier.

"This clever lad is the father of the doomsday machine. He may come in handy someday."

Stretch and Plug seized the prisoner and dragged him off.

TWENTY-SIX

Uma couldn't sleep. Nobody had seen Hubert or Hodja since the previous morning, and she was worried sick. She opened the drawer in her nightstand, brought out the pinwheel he gave her, and sent it spinning with a puff of air. The wheel seemed like such a harmless invention, she thought. How could it possibly have led to so much trouble?

Uma's quality of life, like that of every other Sumerian, had really gone down the tubes since the day of the Assyrian chariot attack. It was all hard labor, all the time. Even worse, Salvo, recalling that she once overcharged him for floor mats, had assigned her a particularly disgusting job: hauling ash.

Sixteen hours a day, she collected the charred remains of the fires that illuminated the vast chambers of the Ziggurat, trundled them out in a wheelbarrow, and added them to the ash heap. The work was hard, smoky, and dangerous, and at the end of her shift, she barely had the energy to drag herself home and collapse into bed.

Uma blew on the pinwheel again and held it up in the moonlight. Through its rotating blades she could see her window, her backyard, and an onager.

An onager?

"Hodja," Uma cried, racing to the window. Sure enough, the faithful beast was standing right outside, his fur matted with sweat from the long run.

"Where's Hubert?"

Hodja did a little dance of panic and frustration. Speech would really be an asset right about now.

"Did he come with you?"

Hodja shook his head.

"Is he in trouble?"

He nodded.

"Is he hurt?"

He shrugged.

"Has he fallen into enemy hands?"

He nodded vigorously.

"Whose hands?"

Hodja cracked his tail like a whip.

"Ajax himself? What happened?"

Well, if he couldn't communicate verbally, he'd just have to act it out. First, he hung his head and tucked his tail between his legs.

"Hubert ran away in shame?" Uma guessed.

Hodja galloped in place.

"He rode all day?"

Hodja mimed drinking a mug of beer, then burped loudly.

"He stopped at the Border Bar and Grill?"

Hodja gyrated like a belly dancer and batted his eyes seductively.

"He disguised himself as an exotic dancer? Hodja, I don't need all the details," she said, frustrated. "Where is Hubert now?"

Hodja crouched low and aimed himself at the distant mountains like a pointer dog.

There was no time to waste. Uma narrowed her eyes in steely resolve. "We have to rescue him."

TWENTY-SEVEN

The sun rose to find Ajax addressing his orderly columns of soldiers.

"Citizens of Assyria, our hour of glory has come at last. No longer shall the noble people of the mountains be forced to live off the crumbs of the selfish pigs of the valley. Today, righteousness shall be restored and vengeance shall be ours!" He'd been practicing the speech all week and delivered it with a great deal of gusto. His soldiers responded with a satisfying, warlike growl.

Ajax uncoiled his whip and cracked it. "Soldiers of Assyria," he trumpeted, "let's move out!" There was a menacing rumble as hundreds of feet, hooves, and wheels were set in motion.

Hubert watched the departure of the army from the stockade, a small jail cell ordinarily reserved for soldiers who violated the Assyrian Code of Military Conduct—which really took some doing.

"There's gotta be some way out of here," he said to Spike as they gazed through the tiny, barred window. Off to their left the giant wheel cast its long, deadly shadow. He'd hoped it would look smaller by daylight, but somehow it seemed even bigger. At its base were Stretch and Plug, who had been posted on the mountain to guard Hubert, as well as to release the weapon at the sound of Ajax's war horn.

For the fiftieth time Hubert tried to pry apart the bars. Solid bronze. For the hundredth time he wondered if Hodja would manage to bring help.

"Psst," said a voice from the other side of the stockade. For the first time since he landed in this hellhole, he felt hope.

Hubert raced to the opposite window, and his heart leapt at the sight of his two friends.

"You came through!" he whispered. "I thought I was dead meat."

"You probably still are," said Uma. "I don't know how to pick locks."

"We'll worry about that later. First we've gotta keep our town from being squashed."

She glanced up at the doomsday machine. "Yeah, Hodja pointed that thing out to me on the way up. What are we gonna do?"

"I have a plan, but you'll have to work fast."

"Me?"

"You can handle it. I'll distract the guards. And Hodja, I'll need your shoes."

"Hodja has shoes?"

"I made him a pair of pants, too, but he never wears them," Hubert said. "Now, here's the plan."

Stretch and Plug knew it would take Ajax and the army a while to reach the city of Ur, so they relaxed in the shade of the doomsday machine and played tic-tac-toe. "Just think," said Stretch. "Before the day's over, that whole valley's gonna be ours."

"First thing I'm gonna do is, go down to the riverbank and drink till I'm ready to pop."

"No, Plug. The first thing you're gonna do at that riverbank is have yourself a bath."

"What's a bath?"

Before Stretch could explain the concept, they were distracted by a rhythmic tapping sound from the stockade. Hustling over to check on their prisoner, the guards were astonished to find Hubert performing an energetic tap-dance routine inside his cell. The horseshoes he'd attached to his feet were kicking up quite a racket on the stone floor.

"What's going on in there?" asked Plug.

"Just working on a combination, fellas," Hubert said through the bars. "Five, six, seven, eight—"

Plug and Stretch looked at each other. They'd heard Sumerians were a little odd but had never witnessed it firsthand.

"Look, you guys still have some time before you destroy my home, family, and friends," Hubert said cheerfully. "If you want, I could teach you a couple of basic steps. Really helps you unwind . . . you know, after a day of marauding and ransacking. It's easy. I'll show you."

Hubert was no Gregory Hines, but he made up for in enthusiasm what he lacked in skill. More importantly, he made a lot of noise—which covered the noise that Uma was making. For unseen by Stretch and Plug, she had tiptoed around behind the wheel and shot a long rope across its top with a bow and arrow left behind by one of the soldiers. After tying one end around Hodja's neck, she looped the other end around her waist. At her signal the onager dug in his hooves and hoisted her clear to the top of the wheel.

Now she was poised high in the air, chipping away at the edge of the doomsday machine with a hammer and chisel. Uma wasn't entirely clear on what purpose this would serve, but she decided just this once to follow Hubert's lead and ask questions later.

Meanwhile, Plug and Stretch, falling prey to rhythm's powerful lure, soon found themselves tapping their little hearts out. Plug showed exceptional promise, mastering the shuffle step and bell kick with grace and ease.

As they clicked away, Hubert whispered in Spike's ear, "Search these guys. Maybe one of them has the key to the stockade." Slithering between the bars, the wily lizard climbed Stretch's leg and darted in and out of his pockets. After searching Plug's pants as well, he returned to Hubert with his haul: a comb, a

used burlap hanky, a withered apple core, and a picture of Plug's mom. No key, though.

"Keep trying," whispered Hubert.

The sun was climbing. Ajax must be nearing the city. At any moment the war horn could blow. Hubert kept dancing, and Spike kept searching, and Uma kept chipping. The plan was a long shot, but it was all they had.

TWENTY-EIGHT

Down in the valley the Town Crier paced the high perimeter of the Ziggurat, keeping watch. To the east he saw nothing; to the south, nothing; to the west, nothing; to the north . . . something! He couldn't be sure what it was, but after that last encounter with the Assyrians, he wasn't taking any chances. "We're under attack!" he cried, then ran to the alarm bell and rank it loud and long.

Everyone in the valley swung into action. Shopkeepers abandoned their wares; mothers herded their kids down the streets; farmers fled their fields. Everybody converged on the Ziggurat, pouring into its dark opening like rats into a tunnel.

Among the surging crowd in the town square, Big Al spotted Gorp.

"Have you seen my daughter?" he hollered over the din.

"No. Any sign of Hubert?" said Gorp. Al shook his head.

Prime Minister Salvo had been running civil defense drills for weeks, and the last citizens were soon safe within the thick walls of the Ziggurat. The heavy gates slammed shut. The children were sent to the innermost chamber for safety, and the soldiers, fully armed, took their assigned places along the wall, ready to withstand whatever trouble lay ahead.

They hoped.

Doggedly, grimly, unceasingly, into the valley of the shadow of the Big Wheel rode the Assyrian army. When they were only a few hundred yards from the Ziggurat, Ajax called a halt. The dust settled, giving the Sumerians up on the battlements their first clear view of the invaders: a compact, well-organized military force outfitted with rolling stock and weapons.

"What shall we do now?" cried Queen Eridu, clutching Salvo's arm.

"Our course of action is clear," said the Prime Minister. "We defend our city to the last man standing. If that means our streets must run with blood, so be it."

"I see," said the Queen. After a moment she added, "Just to play devil's advocate here, Salvo, what if we took a slightly *different* course of action?"

"And what does Your Majesty have in mind?"

"Well, I was thinking, it might be a great deal less . . . messy if we were to sort of . . . throw in the towel and let the Assyrians run things for a while."

"Let me handle this, will you?"

"Oh, dear."

Leaving the rest of the troops behind, Ajax and Karp drove up to the Ziggurat in the lead chariot, halting directly below Salvo and the Queen. Ajax cracked his whip savagely and proclaimed, "In the name of the noble and long-suffering people of Assyria, I command to you to surrender and yield your lands and possessions!" This felt somehow incomplete, so he added, "Or else!"

"Or else what?" challenged the Prime Minister.

"You don't want to find out, bub."

"Oh, my," said the Queen, wringing her hands.

Salvo strode to the railing and put his military mind to work. Gazing out on the plain, he calculated the enemy's troop strength, divided it by his own troop strength, multiplied that figure by the square root of the thickness of the Ziggurat's walls, added his home-court advantage, subtracted Ajax's element of surprise, corrected for wind direction and air temperature—and concluded that there was no need to yield to this thug's demands.

"You can't scare me, caveman," he sneered. "We haven't exactly been sitting on our hands down here. We're armed to the teeth!"

"Nevertheless. I'm giving you one last chance, Salvo. Surrender, or I reduce you to rubble."

"Don't make me laugh. You couldn't conquer a saucer of milk."

"Could, too."

"Could not."

"'Fraid so."

This was going nowhere. Salvo cut to the chase. "Give it your best shot, pal."

"Okay, you asked for it."

Ajax twisted his face into an evil leer. Opening the glove compartment of his chariot, he brought out a long, twisted ram's horn, raised it to his mouth, took a deep breath, and let fly a mighty blast that echoed across the valley. Birds took flight; dogs howled; scorpions scurried into their holes. Then all was quiet again.

"Not bad," Salvo said. "What do you do for an encore?"

"You'll find out," Ajax said. And with that, he turned the chariot around and rode back out of the square.

TWENTY-NINE

Plug and Stretch were on the verge of mastering the time step when the resounding boom of Ajax's war horn jerked them back to reality.

"Sorry, kid," Stretch said. "Gotta go."

"I think we ought to review those kick ball changes, guys. You know, really lock it in." But the guards were already hightailing it to their posts.

Hubert looked to the top of the wheel. How in the world was Uma going to get down from there? She wouldn't have time to descend by rope; Stretch and Plug were hauling on the blocks and tackle, and the chocks were inching out. If only he could get out of this cell. . . .

For once luck lent a hand. When Stretch bent forward to give his rope another pull, the outline of the stockade key became visible in his pants.

"Left rear pocket," Hubert told Spike, and flung him between the cell bars. Spike hit the ground running, streaked over to Stretch, and with a mighty effort managed to extract the key—but not before the chocks were pulled clear, and the wheel started to move.

Uma's eyes locked on Hubert's as the massive weapon began to quake beneath her feet.

Now their future was in Spike's tiny reptilian hands. Clenching the key in his mouth, the lizard blazed across the open ground, scaled the stockade door, and dropped it in Hubert's outstretched palm.

Within seconds the prisoner was free. He sprang onto Hodja's back, and together they charged directly into the weapon's path.

The wheel had completed a quarter turn by now, throwing Uma into a forward free fall. There was nothing between her and the hard ground below but thin air—and one highly determined sixteen-year-old inventor riding a small but scrappy onager.

Had the catch that Hubert made happened five thousand years later, it would no doubt have been compared with Willy Mays's celebrated basket catch, which robbed the Cleveland Indians' Vic Wertz of extra bases in the first game of the 1954 World Series. But occurring way back when it did, you'd just have to call it . . . incomparable.

"Oof," said Uma, Hubert, Hodja, and Spike simultaneously, and the quartet sped down the hill just ahead of the rapidly descending wheel. Hodja went into overdrive, staying scant inches ahead of their unstoppable pursuer until he spotted a side path, ducked

into it, and screeched to a halt as the doomsday device thundered past.

The fate of Sumeria now depended entirely on Hubert's plan.

Naturally, all these heroic acts weren't visible from the Ziggurat. But pretty soon the wheel was.

"Salvo," said the Queen, tapping him on the shoulder, "it would appear that one of those mountain peaks is headed our way."

Squinting at the horizon, Salvo quickly figured out

what was in store. Drat. Those pesky Assyrians were smarter than he thought.

A menacing rumble could soon be felt, then heard. A wave of terror passed through every Sumerian. There was no time to flee through the Ziggurat's narrow exits; they were all sitting ducks, trapped in the very building to which they had fled for safety.

Ajax, who had stationed himself and his troops at a safe distance from the imminent carnage, laughed maniacally at this delicious irony—his second today. The deadly juggernaut sped across the valley floor toward its target. In a moment the entire Tigris-Euphrates Valley would be his to enjoy—after peeling up all those flat Sumerians, of course. But his joy faded as he noticed something: The wheel was changing direction!

Ajax shot Colonel Karp an accusing look. "Who aimed that thing?"

"You did, sir," answered Karp with a gulp.

But there was no doubt about the weapon's faulty trajectory. It was definitely veering to one side. If it continued to follow this course, it would completely miss the Ziggurat. Come to think of it, it was headed straight for—

"RUN!" yelled Ajax.

Watching from his high vantage point in the Zagros Mountains, Hubert was jubilant. "You did it," he said to Uma as he pounded her back in congratulations. "By reducing the circumference of one lateral face of a cylinder relative to the other, you transformed its shape into that of a conic section!"

Uma, Hodja, and Spike were totally baffled.

"Sorry. What I mean is, you chipped away enough of one edge to make it curve to the side. You know. Like what it's doing."

"I knew that," Uma said.

Now it was the Assyrians' turn to panic. The wheel was headed directly for Ajax and his army like a runaway freight train. He prayed for a miracle.

He got one.

Between Ajax and the speeding weapon lay a small hill, a geographic irregularity in the otherwise flat Sumerian landscape. Functioning like a ski jump, it launched the wheel skyward. Like a crowd at a slow-motion tennis match, everyone in the valley turned his head in unison and gasped as the immense hunk of granite zoomed over Ajax's head, momentarily blocking out the sun, and landed with a cataclysmic splash in a gorge in the Euphrates River.

And plugged it up.

For perhaps the first time in Mesopotamian history, every single citizen had the same thought: "Now what?"

THIRTY

A life-threatening crisis has a way of drawing people together, or at least of making them temporarily forget they can't stomach each other. So when the Sumerians and Assyrians assembled next to the dry riverbed, it was not as rivals or warring factions, but as a large group of Mesopotamians deprived of their only source of water. It was almost as if a truce had been called.

Salvo quickly broke it. "I hope you're satisfied," he told Ajax. "Now we're high and dry."

"Hey, buddy," Ajax countered, "if you flatlanders had been willing to share a little water, maybe let us plant some chickpeas once in a while, we never would've gone on the attack."

They faced off like a pair of Sumo wrestlers.

"Well, now *nobody* has any water, you Neanderthal."

"Well, it's not my fault. And keep my relatives out of it."

"Well, it most certainly isn't *my* fault."

"Oh, no? Then whose fault is it?"

Hubert conveniently chose this moment to come riding up, with Uma behind him.

"Wow," he said. "Close call, huh?"

This comment was met by stony silence from the citizenry, who, of course, had no way of knowing that he had just saved all their necks.

"Something the matter?" asked Hubert.

"Allow me to summarize," said Queen Eridu, stepping to the fore. "I believe I speak for everyone present when I say that were it not for your little invention, we wouldn't be in our current predicament."

He dismounted and glanced down into the dry riverbed. "What, that? No problem, Your Highness. After all, you can't stop a river. When the water level gets high enough, it'll just trickle around the sides of the dam, and everything'll go on like before."

This made sense. The Queen breathed a sigh of relief. "Of course. You're right. So there's really nothing to worry about."

Just then the wheel shuddered ominously, shifting under the increasing weight of the water behind it. "Not as long as it holds, anyway," Hubert added.

"Oh, dear," she said.

THIRTY-ONE

Death by tidal wave in the middle of a desert. This was a new one. The Queen racked her brain for a solution but came up empty.

"Does anybody have any ideas?" she asked in desperation.

Nobody spoke, but Hubert's mind was already racing. Behind him millions of gallons of water were gathering. In front of him was the entire Tigris-Euphrates Valley, including the helpless city of Ur and thousands of people whose lives and futures depended on what happened next.

"I do," he said.

"Right," said Queen Eridu. "Does anyone *else* have an idea?"

Ajax raised his hand. "I've got one. Why don't we pile up all the Sumerians against the dam, and the rest of us can get out of here while there's still time?"

"I've got a better one," Salvo said. "Why don't you wrap that big mouth of yours around that big wheel you made . . . and swallow it?"

Ajax made a fist and shook it under Salvo's nose. "Why, I oughta . . ."

Hubert had to do something fast, before a brawl started. He stepped up onto a rock to plead his case. "Look, I know most of you don't have much faith in me right now, and I can't say I blame you. But I think I can solve this problem."

Spotting his father among the dubious audience, Hubert spoke directly to him. "I know I can. And I'm asking you—just this one last time—to trust me."

Gorp looked hard at his son. He saw a pest, a troublemaker, a loose cannon . . . but something else as well. Gorp saw a confident, brave young man on the verge of adulthood. He saw the spirit of Samarra, whose creativity, he understood, was the best part of her, even if he didn't understand creativity. And he even saw a little of himself: stubborn, determined, in it for the long haul, and when push came to shove (as it so often did in Gorp's line of work), undeniably . . . trustworthy.

"I trust you," Gorp said.

No one spoke as the hauler lumbered through the crowd and stood at his son's side. Hubert tried to say a few words of thanks, but some kind of lump seemed to be stuck in his throat.

Salvo broke the silence. "Yeah, yeah, yeah. I'm deeply touched. So now that we've had our little male bonding moment, let me remind everyone that this hooligan has about as much credibility as a seven-shekel coin, and anybody who takes his advice is just as nuts as he is."

The wheel shifted another inch. The crowd was on the verge of panic. Hubert was about to jump out of his skin. He knew how to solve the problem, but how could he possibly get these people to listen? Salvo was only interested in power, and Ajax was only interested in conquest, and the Queen was only interested in astrology, and . . .

Astrology. That was it.

He cleared his throat and addressed Salvo, who stood with arms folded, practically drooling at the prospect of battle. "That's not a very nice way to talk to a guy on his birthday," he said. Then Hubert stole a glance at the Queen. As he'd hoped, her eyes suddenly lit up.

"Your birthday?"

Gorp, confused, started to speak, but Hubert silenced him with a swift kick to the shin. "That's right, Your Highness."

"So that would make you . . ."

"An Aquarius."

Queen Eridu took a step backward, visibly shaken. "Aquarius. The Water Bearer," she cried, raising her scepter heavenward. "*It's an omen!*"

Galvanized by the Queen's enthusiasm, the crowd began to chatter excitedly. Uma stepped over to Hubert. "I thought you were born in July," she said under her breath. He just gave her an innocent smile.

Uma raised her eyebrows. "That was a total lie," she whispered.

"You call it a lie. I call it giving the customers what they want."

Queen Eridu's shimmering robes flashed in the sunlight as she stepped up next to Hubert and raised his hand like a winning prizefighter's. "Fate speaks in mysterious ways, and as it has chosen to speak on this day through this young man, I command all of you, as your omnipotent ruler, to do his bidding, whatever it may be."

"Wait a minute," Salvo protested. "Do you mean to tell me I don't get to fight my war because some kid is an Aquarius?"

"Sorry, dearie," said the Queen.

Salvo had skulked too long and hard to sit still for this. "As Supreme Commander of the Armed Forces," he shouted, "I order my troops to defend our Sumerian homeland against these odious scoundrels."

"But what about the dam?" asked a concerned Sumerian.

"Damn the dam," Salvo said, leaping aboard the nearest steed and raising his sword. "It's hammer time! Charge!"

Salvo's charge would have been much more effective if the steed he happened to leap aboard hadn't been Hodja. The onager gave a snort of surprise,

charged straight to the edge of the empty riverbed, and hit the brakes, catapulting the Prime Minister right down the bank. There followed a longish series of thumps, bangs, yelps, and curses, then silence. The crowd gave a shrug and turned its attention back to the Queen and Hubert.

"Right, then," she said. "Now tell us, oh Water Bearer—for that shall henceforth be thy true and only name—by what wondrous method do you plan to bear this water away?"

"Well, we'll need shovels. And picks. And lots and lots of people. Oh, and I'll need something to draw with."

She solemnly offered the Water Bearer her scepter. "It is so decreed," she decreed.

Gorp put his hand on Hubert's shoulder. There was much to be said, but this clearly wasn't the time to say it. There was work to do.

"How can I help?" Gorp said.

Hubert smiled shyly. "Well, I could really use my toolbox right about now."

For the next several hours Hubert seemed to be everywhere at once: designing, building, measuring, calculating, hammering, sawing, and giving instructions to work crews up and down the river.

"The trenches should be about three feet deep . . . keep digging due north until you meet up with the team coming from the west . . . the gates need to be at least twenty feet wide . . . we can use these logs for reinforcements . . . don't worry about making it pretty, we can clean things up later."

Diggers dug; tunnelers tunneled; hod carriers carried hods; bricklayers laid bricks; woodworkers worked wood. Wheels were employed everywhere, in wheelbarrows, block and tackle, pulleys, carts, chariots.

Every able-bodied man, woman, and child toiled side by side—they no longer thought of themselves as Sumerians or Assyrians, but simply as Mesopotamians. Even Cliff, Jiff, and Dirk proved useful. For once, their brash confidence came in handy—if a job required dangling by a rope from a high precipice, they were right there, no questions asked.

Everyone gave his all in the joint struggle against their common enemy: time.

THIRTY-TWO

The sun was low in the sky by the time the project was completed. And not a moment too soon—a tremendous reservoir had backed up for miles behind the dam, which was now visibly quaking under the strain. Hubert stood atop it, the destiny of an entire people in his hands.

It was, as the Royal Sportscasters might have put it, a high-pressure situation.

To Hubert's right and left, Gorp and Big Al, each manning a crank connected to a big sluice gate, awaited his orders. The moment of truth had arrived.

"Now!" yelled Hubert.

Gorp and Al turned the cranks.

The gates opened.

With a mighty roar, twin cataracts of white water filled the flood channels that flanked the dam, then continued along deep channels next to the riverbed. Each channel divided into smaller trenches, which divided into tributaries, which divided into a vast grid of orderly ditches that fanned out across the flat, dry valley.

The plan worked. The dam held. The water went where it was supposed to go.

Not only had Hubert saved a city and thousands of people, but he had invented irrigation.

A cheer went up from the masses. No one had ever witnessed anything like this before—except, of course, Hodja, who had seen the basic principles laid out in the backyard on the day Hubert invented plumbing.

Watching from a high bluff were Ajax and Queen Eridu, who, having forgotten that they were at war as recently as this morning, breathed a joint sigh of relief.

"I must say," she said, "you Assyrians aren't nearly as beastly as I'd been led to believe."

"Thanks, Queen. You're not so bad yourself."

"Please, call me Eridu."

"Only if you call me Ajax."

"You know, Ajax, with so much new arable land, perhaps we can grow enough food for *all* our people."

"I was just thinking the same thing!" said the former warlord, taking note for the first time of how very stylish the Sumerian Queen looked in purple.

She gazed into his eyes. "Really! Tell me something, Jaxy . . . what's your sign?"

Hubert and Gorp stood on the bank of the placidly flowing Euphrates. Above them the twin spillways arced gracefully on either side of the new dam. The wheel was considerably less threatening when it wasn't screaming down on you at a hundred miles an hour.

"I've gotta hand it to you, kid, you did one heck of a job here," Gorp said. "If only your mom could see this . . . I know just what she'd say."

"Yeah, me too—"

They were interrupted by a piercing scream. It was too high to be clearly understood, but it sounded something like "Look out beloooooooooowww!"

Hubert and Gorp looked up toward the dam, where they saw something remarkable—even by the remarkable standards of this remarkable day.

What they saw was a log shooting through the sluice gate, sailing past them, and plunging into the water below.

Straddling the log was Samarra.

That's right. Gorp's wife. Hubert's mother. The creative, long-lost, presumed-dead Samarra.

That one.

"Honey bunch?" said Gorp.

"Mom?" said Hubert.

Later, wrapped in a blanket at the river's edge, Samarra explained what had happened back on that fateful, windy day. After soaring mile after mile dangling from the umbrella pole, she had crash-landed on a remote ledge high above the river. As it was impossible to climb up or down the sheer cliff, Samarra had remained stranded there all this time. It was a hard, lonely existence, but she survived on the hope that one day she'd see her family again. She also survived on roots, berries, and the occasional stray buzzard. She would still have been there but for that sudden, mysterious rise in the river that brought her the log on which she made her escape.

"By the way, what's that big round thing?" she asked, pointing to the dam.

Hubert and Gorp smiled at each other. "It's a long story, Mom," Hubert said.

EPILOGUE

Six months later all the Assyrians had relocated from the mountains to the fertile valley, where, as the Queen had foretold, there would surely be plenty of food for everybody. The irrigated fields were green with the first new crops, and Ur was fast becoming the hub of civilization. Paddleboats plied the waters of the Tigris and Euphrates, spinning windmills dotted the horizon, and waterwheel-driven factories lined the riverbanks.

Queen Eridu and Ajax were married in a simple ceremony attended by six bridesmaids, six grooms-men, and the entire population of the world as they knew it.

The Town Crier announced a few months later that the Royal Couple were expecting a child, and were considering the name Hubert if it was a boy, or if it was a girl, Hubertina.

The Ziggurat was restored to its original purpose, a community center to be enjoyed by all the people of Mesopotamia.

Salvo, who had sustained a nasty broken leg while

tumbling down the riverbank, was removed from his position as Prime Minister and given the less-demanding job of Royal Groundskeeper. He spent his days puttering in the Garden of Peace and Freedom in a special wheelchair Hubert built for him, and found he had a knack for raising prizewinning lilacs.

Big Al continued to expand his share of the carriage trade, pioneering such concepts as rack-and-pinion steering, disk brakes, and zero-percent financing.

Stretch and Plug perfected a crowd-pleasing tap

routine and were soon appearing two nights a week at the Border Bar & Grill.

Gorp and Samarra picked up where they'd left off, enjoying a peaceful domestic life in which he did the towing and hauling and she did the cooking and inventing. She continued to perfect the umbrella (working only on calm days) and, as a tribute to her brilliant son, created a flat cracker shaped like a wheel, which she named the "Euphrates."

Hubert kept right on inventing, too, but he took a somewhat broader view now, having learned a thing or two since that day down by the riverbank. From Uma he learned that an idea doesn't sell itself, no matter how good it is; from Ajax and Salvo, that new technology can have unexpected consequences and must be handled with the utmost care; from his father, that even the most stubborn person can change with the times; and from himself, that one person with one idea can change the world.

"So, what's your next project?" Uma asked Hubert one day as they strolled through the park where they had gone on their first date. (Hodja was up ahead, pushing Spike on the merry-go-round.)

"Well, I never did quite get that mousetrap right."

"A mousetrap? You've gotta be kidding."

"Actually, it's kind of been weighing on my mind."

"I guess I was expecting something a little more ambitious."

They stopped for a moment next to the new half-pipe, where Cliff, Jiff, and Dirk were trying out moves on Hubert's latest creation, the skateboard. "I figure the world's always going to need a better mousetrap," he said. "But this whole wheel craze—I mean, how long do you think it can last?"

Uma raised her eyes to the horizon. "Well, Hubert, you never know."